WHO OKAYED THIS?!

THE RIVETING LIFE OF GRANT DAVIS

PHILIP E. BARRINGTON

Who Okayed This?! The Riveting Life of Grant Davis.
Copyright © 2021 by Philip E. Barrington
Edited by Virginia Aronson

First Edition

Hardcover ISBN: 978-1-64990-576-5
Paperback ISBN: 978-1-64990-931-2
eBook ISBN: 978-1-64990-190-3

PROLOGUE

I woke up in the land of sunshine and palm trees. I didn't know if I was really awake or still dreaming.

As I lay there on the couch, I heard the birds chirping. Then a new sound emerged from the bedroom. *Clunk, drag, clunk, drag.* What the hell was that?

A booming voice called out "Good morning!" And my mother's walker continued to drag across the floor.

I realized I was on her couch, staying at her condo in Florida. What the hell was I doing there?

Your guess was as good as mine.

I needed a cup of hazelnut coffee to figure things out.

I prepared my favorite coffee using the precise scoops per cup and the perfect amount of spring water. There was only one thing left to do. Press the *on* button.

The sound of the coffeemaker and the aroma of hazelnut enveloped the kitchen, as well as the dining room, living room, and bathroom. My mom lived in a condo the size of a shoebox. But there was plenty of sunshine gleaming through all the windows. This gave me some kind of hope and inspiration.

As I was drinking my first cup of coffee and the caffeine began coursing through my veins, everything started coming back to me. As it came into focus, I put it all in perspective.

CHAPTER 1

THE BEGINNING

My name is Grant Davis. I was born in Brooklyn, New York, and raised on Long Island. I was a junior model for a well-known department store. My father was in the real estate and insurance business and my mom was a homemaker. We lived in a nice upper-middle-class neighborhood, where the skies were blue and the schools safe. Everything was great!

My dad's business was thriving and life was cotton candy and lollipops. Until one day my dad got sick. He developed pneumonia and landed in the hospital. He wound up staying there for six months.

His partner and so called friend Manny, the maintenance man of all the buildings my father managed, had a gambling problem. While my dad was out sick, Manny got nothing done. He spent money that was not his on gambling

When my father recovered, he discovered there were liens and judgments against him. My dad had trusted Manny because my father loved people and people really loved him. My dad felt that deep down inside people were generally good, that all of us meant well and had good intentions.

My dad had made the mistake of not hiring a professional management company. Manny mismanaged everything, mainly by not handling anything. Instead, he spent his time visiting the track, betting on horses, hiring call girls, and taking frequent trips to Atlantic City. All with money that did not belong to him.

With friends like Manny, who needed enemies?

So, when my father recovered and was discharged from the hospital, he was forced to fold up his business. He went back to college to earn a masters' degree in music education. Then he became a struggling substitute teacher on Long Island.

Once a person is over a certain age, it becomes quite difficult to obtain a job as a teacher, as my father soon found out. So he also had gigs at various nightclubs, where he played piano. He also taught piano privately.

For obvious reasons, my stay-at-home mother went back into the workforce. She got a fulltime job as a secretary for a camera manufacturer.

MY DAD

My father was born in Brooklyn in 1932. He grew up across the street from Ebbets Field, where the Brooklyn Dodgers once played. He used to watch them all the time. The Brooklyn Dodgers were around before the Yankees or the Mets.

My dad used to find baseballs outside the stadium from all the homeruns they made. When he was a kid, my dad enjoyed playing handball on the steps with his friends.

Life wasn't all fun, though. He had bright red hair that really stood out. He also had a lot of freckles, and very large ears like an elephant. Okay, maybe not quite like an elephant, but very noticeable, and this made him self-conscious. It didn't matter, though, because the girls thought he was cute.

One day a bunch of kids were picking on Clint, a little kid my dad knew from the neighborhood. Now, my dad knew what it was like to be picked on. Clint was small, much smaller than a lot of the other kids, but he was always nice to my dad. So, my dad got in the middle of all the bullying. He said to a kid named Walter, "Why don't you pick on someone your own size?" Then my dad socked Walter in the eye, and kicked him when he was on the ground. He told Walter to scram before he mopped up the streets with him.

Walter got up and ran away.

Clint thanked my dad. He asked, "Billy, why did you help me?"

My dad said, "I'm tired of watching these monsters harass you. They take your lunch money all the time. It's not fair."

Clint thanked my dad again, they shook hands, and they both went home to their parents because it was dinnertime.

Clint became an attorney, and he practiced entertainment law. He eventually became one of the largest music producers in the industry. He produced and managed some of the biggest stars in the music world today. He became a mogul well-known throughout the industry as a man who helped countless people become music success stories.

When my dad came home from fighting in the Korean War, he worked as an opera singer as well as a pianist. He also worked as a ballroom dance instructor for many years. He served as the president of his glee club in Brooklyn. He was theatrical, a member of the theater wing in New York City for many years.

He enjoyed meeting people. I mean, he really loved people! It was important for him to be liked and have friends.

My mother, on the other hand, was skeptical of everybody, and in her eyes all of them were guilty until proven innocent. This attitude drove my dad up a wall. They came from two different schools of thought. My dad was an extrovert with hundreds of friends, and my mom was an introvert with very few friends.

They were exact opposites, but they loved each other and were married for over forty years.

RUNAWAY

Every summer my friends went to sleep-away camp. Many of my friends came from wealthy families. They would tour Egypt or visit the rainforests of the Amazon, going on safari or chewing on cacao leaves. They all went to the Disneyworld in Orlando, Florida, every year with their families. I was the only kid in the neighborhood who had never been there. I watched the parade on television every year, wishing and dreaming I was there like all the other kids. I wanted to know what the Florida sun felt like.

I'd never seen a palm tree, except on TV.

One winter I had a brilliant idea. It was so cold; there was snow on the ground and all around. The trees were filled with ice and the cars had to drive through slush. I decided to take a bus to California. I had a little money saved up from my Bar Mitzvah, and the tickets were cheap. My best friend Larry had just moved to California with his parents. I figured I would surprise him when I arrived at his door.

It was freezing outside when I took a cab to the bus station. I purchased a one-way ticket to San Diego and hopped aboard. I thought how I would finally have the chance to see the countryside.

It took me six days to get to California. We stopped every six hours to gas up or switch buses. When we reached Ohio, I fell asleep at a bus terminal in front of the TV. At the time it cost twenty-five cents for fifteen minutes and one dollar for an hour to watch shows on a miniature television.

The bus took off without me.

When I woke up, I had to board another bus. This bus was taking a different route. So, I wound up zigzagging across the country all the way to California.

On the new bus, a priest sat next to me. He noticed the cross I wore around my neck and said, "Hello there, I'm Father Paul."

"Hello, I'm Grant."

"The cross you're wearing, where is it from?"

"It's from Lourdes."

"Grant, were you born a Christian?"

I wasn't. "No," I replied.

"So why are you wearing a cross around your neck?"

"I started meditating a few months ago and it changed my life. I also find Christian people to be more compassionate and kind."

He looked pleased.

I said, "Let me show you something." I took off the cross and showed it to him. "Look in the back. There's a vial of water. It's healing water from France."

The priest nodded. "Oh yes, I've heard of this place and the holy water from there." He turned to me and asked, "Do you believe in Jesus?"

"Yes," I replied.

"Have you been baptized?"

"No."

"Would you like to be? Right now?"

"Yes! But there's no water, don't we need water?"

Father Paul said, "The water inside your cross will work as long as you're wearing it."

Then he baptized me right there, on the bus. Afterwards, everybody on the bus stood up and clapped their hands, and then they all congratulated me. Even the bus driver pulled over to stand up and clap.

When Father Paul reached his destination, he instructed the bus driver to watch over me all the way to California, which he did.

I watched out the window as the terrain changed. The mountains were beautiful, full of snow, and the landscape was just like a painting.

By the time we reached the west coast, some of the people on the bus suspected I was a runaway. Someone reported me to the police.

When we pulled into the terminal in Los Angeles, the police were waiting for me at the bus stop. When I stepped off the bus, the cops pulled me aside and questioned me. They told frightening stories of runaway kids getting hurt or killed. Then they gave me the option to continue running or to go with them.

I certainly did not want to end up like one of the kids they'd described. So I went with them. I felt it was the smart choice.

I wound up at the Beverly Hills Police Department, where the cops called my dad. He answered the phone.

"Hello there, sir, this is the Beverly Hills Police Department."

"Why is the Beverly Hills Police Department calling me?" my dad asked indirectly.

The cop said, "Do you have a son named Grant?"

My dad said yes.

"I have some good news, sir. Your son is here with us!"

"What's my son doing in Beverly Hills?"

"Your guess is as good as ours, sir."

The police placed me in an orphanage for the evening. There was one kid there. Bruno invited me to go out to Hollywood and Vine to mess with all the hookers.

I said, "No, I'm too tired."

He had a wild and crazy look, that kid.

STAR GAZING

The next morning a detective came to pick me up. We got in his Lincoln Town Car to drive to the airport. When we arrived at the airport he gave me a look. "Don't let me find out you skipped this flight. Because when I get hold of you after that, I won't be so nice. If you know what I mean."

I did. "I'll be on that flight, sir!"

That afternoon, I boarded a 747 heading to NYC.

During the flight, I became restless. I was in an aisle next to this lady who would not keep quiet, not even for a second. I noticed all the center row seats were empty, except for one where a man was seated. So, I decided to move there. I needed to stretch, and I needed some space to do this.

A flight attendant came over and asked me to return to my assigned seat. She said, "All of these seats were reserved by that gentleman."

She pointed to the guy and he looked up from his paperwork. "Leave him be!" he told her. He gave me a look. Then he said, "Hey kid, you look hungry. Do you want something to eat?"

I nodded my head.

He told the stewardess, "The gentleman over there, he'll have a turkey dinner with all the trimmings, and a large glass of milk."

I said, "Wow, thank you!"

He replied, "No problem, kid, but I can't talk to you right now, I'm working."

He had a bunch of papers spread out in in front of him.

I nodded. "I understand."

After I had finished my dinner, the man looked over at me and said, "Hey, kid, you want some dessert?"

I was hungry but I didn't want to take advantage of him. So I just shrugged.

He called over the stewardess and said, "The gentleman will now have ice cream. One scoop of every kind you've got, with whipped cream, hot fudge, and don't forget the cherry on top." He laughed and said to me, "Kid, the cherry's the best part."

I agreed. "You're right!"

The stewardess whispered in my ear, "You sure are lucky. Do you know who that is?"

I replied, "A really nice man."

She said, "It's not every day things like this happen. You're one of the lucky ones."

I smiled at the nice man and said, "Thank you, sir."

A short while later, the plane touched ground and we exited together. He ruffled my hair and said, "I'll see you around. Take care!"

My parents were waiting for me. They looked at me funny as I thanked the man again for everything and waved goodbye.

He gave me a grin and said, "It was nice meeting you, kid!" He had a twinkle in his eye. Then he put on his sunglasses and walked to a waiting limousine.

The man had longish hair, and he was handsome. He was tan, dressed well, and acted suave and super charming. He possessed a certain something, a special *it* quality.

When I hurried over to my parents, they were jumping up and down. I thought they were wildly happy to see me home safe. They were, but their excitement was because they were star struck. They were more excited about seeing me with the nice man than they were about getting me home in one piece.

My father said, "Grant, do you know who that man is?"

I replied, "No?"

My mother said, "He's one of the most famous actors in the world! Why was he talking with you?"

I said, "He gave me one of his seats. The aisle seat was stuffy! He also bought me dinner and desert. He thought I looked hungry."

My dad said, "If I didn't see this with my own eyes, I would never believe it!"

My parents went crazy, both of them hysterically laughing. They said they couldn't wait to tell all their friends.

The next day, my parents took me to the opening of a new movie. As the film began, there he was on the screen, my friend from the plane. He was the star of the movie! It was hard to believe this man I had met, the guy who bought me dinner, was up on the silver screen and millions of people all over the world knew who he was.

What a strange and wonderful world it was.

Well, that did it for me. I'd always be a fan!

As for Larry, he never knew I was on my way to San Diego. In fact, he didn't even know I'd run away.

CHAPTER 2

BOARDING SCHOOL

After my on the road adventure, I was informed that I would be going away to boarding school. My parents had arranged for me to go to school in the Catskill Mountains in upstate New York.

I packed my things, and I was off.

It was crisp and beautiful up in the mountains. The leaves were changing colors and the smell of a roaring fireplace was in the air.

The boarding school was on a large estate. It looked like a castle made of stone, and that's exactly what it was. The estate had a history. The stones were imported from Europe, from an original castle, and rebuilt. The builders had reproduced the castle, piling up the stones in precisely the same order but in the Catskills.

Before it was a school, priests and cardinals resided there. There was another stone structure where the nuns had once lived. There were many acres of land with small cottages that were used as learning annexes. The property was quite beautiful.

In the rear of the main estate, where I lived, I could watch the most beautiful sunsets. As I looked off into the distance, I could see mountains layered by other mountains, and it went on for miles. That's where the sun would set.

The teachers were all different with different teaching styles. The students were from all over the country. A few were from my hometown. That gave me some comfort.

MUSIC TEACHERS

My music teachers were the best. Milton, my main music teacher, was a Tibetan Buddhist who had practiced for more than thirty years. He was also an amazing jazz musician. He had his own trio.

Milton had one requirement before class started. We had to follow him through a series of chi kung exercises, to help channel our energies into music. I loved that.

My other music teacher played as many horned instruments as Milton. Robert had white hair and a white beard, and he always wore a peace symbol. He told the class about the importance of meditation. "Practicing keeps your mind clear and your thinking straight." He liked us to meditate using colors and geometrical shapes.

One day Robert mentioned he was friends with a famous member of the most famous band in the world. Robert had been around, traveling within the music circuits, way before I was born. But I was a skeptic so I wasn't sure I believed him.

Years later, I was researching in order to do a thesis on this musician. I came across an old photograph of a poster for an event. The event was hosted by this person, and the poster listed the names of all the well-known rock stars expected to attend. Robert's name was on that list.

Did I have cool teachers or what?

My English teacher was really nice. Claire told me she used to be a hippy, but she had grown up and become straight-laced. A fellow student felt the need to torture this nice woman. Adam liked to disrupt the classroom on a constant basis. He would make fun of Claire. One day he shot a fire extinguisher at her. He was crazy.

Needless to say, Adam was never allowed back into her classroom, or any of the others for that matter. He was expelled and sent home. After that, there was peace in Claire's classroom.

Then one day we were sitting in class and Claire seemed…different. I asked Dennis, who sat next to me, if something strange was going on with her.

He said, "Yeah, she's stoned out of her mind!"

We laughed.

After class, Dennis said to Claire, "Grant and I know you're stoned. So share some of your bud with us."

Claire shook her head and said no, she wasn't stoned. Then she smiled and walked away. As she put on her sunglasses, she giggled softly.

A few days later, Claire's husband and stepson were scheduled to come to campus to visit her. They planned to have lunch and take a walk on the grounds. Claire told me, "My stepson is an actor."

That intrigued me.

Claire's family pulled up in a new Jeep. Claire's husband Charles was smoking a wood pipe and he wore old-fashioned suspenders. Her stepson wore an army jacket. He was quiet, low key, not looking for attention.

At the time, he was not yet famous. Today he's a major celebrity. He plays one of my favorite superheroes. Let's just say he's not the man of steel but the man of....?

See how cool my teachers were?

My favorite substitute teacher, Russ, was an ex-beatnik. He loved to play the harmonica. Russ listened to all types of music.

One weekend I was invited to stay with Russ and his family. When Russ picked me up from school on Friday afternoon, he said, "Grant, I'm going to drop you off in town for a little while. My wife and I have to clean up the house before you come over."

"That's fine," I replied.

He dropped me off in a nearby village, where colonies of artists had gathered for nearly two centuries. Artists of all kinds gathered there every year.

I walked to the local pizzeria and had a couple of slices, washing them down with a root beer. Then I walked around town. I went into all the little shops, and soon enough Russ was there looking for me.

When I jumped into his car, he smiled and turned on some rock 'n' roll, then put on his sunglasses. He said his family was home cooking dinner, and we needed to be there on time. When we arrived at his house, dinner was still in the oven cooking. Russ and I went into his living room and sat down.

I said, "Russ, I know you're married, but I've seen how much the women like you. How come the girls gravitate to you?"

Russ laughed. "Do you really want to know?"

"Yes," I replied.

Russ told me he came from San Francisco. "I was taught at a very early age to always, no matter what, be honest, sincere, and open about your feelings. I am, and people pick up on my sincerity. Especially women! During the late sixties, I was in charge of public activities in San Francisco, including serving as the coordinator for many free love events. Those led to many private gatherings," he said with a shy smile.

"Private gatherings?" I asked.

"Yes, they were my specialty. I was the master of ceremonies, the conductor of many, many wild orgies." He laughed.

I was blown away. I couldn't believe my ears. Orgies?

"How in the world did you do that?" I asked.

"How in the world was I the master of ceremonies or the conductor of orgies? Or both?" he asked with a twinkle in his eye.

I shrugged, sitting forward in my chair. To my surprise, he laughed and went into a long description of his activities in San Francisco. I was riveted.

On our way to dinner, I promised him I would never reveal what he had shared. After all, he worked at the school as a substitute teacher.

Russ's wife cooked up a wonderful dinner, accompanied by a fabulous dessert. Later that evening, Russ said, "Grant, I'm going to blast some music in the morning, so you better wake up early!"

I thought he was joking.

Early Saturday morning, I was blasted out of bed by a stereo system. When I arrived in the living room, my hands covering my ears, Russ laughed. He told me he played the same album every morning. He played it religiously, like a ritual, a famous German musical that was on Broadway.

Strange choice for wakeup music!

Russ said, "I warned you!" Then he smiled and made himself a grapefruit juice and vodka cocktail. He drank it while listening to the musical, as if we were in a music appreciation class.

He did this every morning.

On Monday morning when he finished his cocktail, Russ put on his sunglasses. Then he turned off the stereo because we were headed back to school. I thanked Russ and his family for having me over for the weekend. But now, I had to get in the car with him.

I put on my seatbelt and strapped myself in.

During the ride back to campus, I told him, "I really like the principal's secretary, Marie."

Russ smiled and asked, "What is it about her that you like?"

"She has these big beautiful eyes, a great big smile, and the sexiest legs to ever walk in high heels," I replied. "Sometimes, I go to the principal's office to visit her, just to say hello."

"Is she the lady with the long blonde hair? The curly hair? She walks around campus on her lunch break all the time?" Russ asked.

When I said yes, Russ growled like a wolf. He said, "Grant, you have good taste! Now you need to let her know how you feel about her. And you better hurry up before I take her back to my lair and devour her."

"You and me both," I replied.

We both laughed.

Then I said, "Marie is mine because you're married."

Russ laughed. "You're right, but my wife and I have an open marriage."

"What does that mean?"

Russ smiled. "It means you better ask Marie out for coffee real soon or I'm going to take her back to my lair for both my wife and I to feast on."

I looked at Russ. He grinned and said, "My wife likes women too."

I sat back in my seat. Wow.

"See, I met my wife at one of the events I was conducting in San Fran. We fell in love, and the rest is history. So you need to go see Marie today. Try telling her how you genuinely feel. Be sincere, you might be delightfully surprised."

I said, "Marie is a dream girl."

"Then go speak with her. With a little luck on your side, your life will soon feel like a dream. You're young, so go get her and have yourself some fun! That's what makes life worth living. If you can't try to live out some of your dreams, what's the point of getting up in the morning?"

I nodded. I was still a kid, but years later I realized how much the advice Russ gave me that day was worth. I took his words to heart.

As for me and Marie, turns out she didn't date students.

MORE SCHOOLS

A year later, my school was sold. I headed back to Long Island.

While I was waiting to be admitted to a new school, I hung out at an arcade in town.

Every Tuesday was biker night and every Thursday was car night, and this made things interesting. There were a lot of interesting people there to chat with.

One day I was talking with this guy and his girlfriend about meditation. Bob and Brenda said they'd tried to meditate a few times but it was too difficult for them. I told them, "The secret is to not try at all."

"How do you not try?"

I replied, "You just observe your thoughts coming and going."

Bob laughed. "That's what we do on our motorcycles. I guess that's why we love riding so much."

We all laughed.

Bob and his girlfriend were great people, honest, direct, and sincere. I complimented them on that.

Bob said, "Grant, my word means everything to me. If you don't have that, you don't have anything in life."

We walked around looking at some of the motorcycles and all the work that went into them. Bob said, "Grant, don't ever give up on your dreams. Don't listen to what other people say, because they only want to see you in their boat. Always follow your dreams!"

Bob was a musician, and he offered me a job as a stagehand. He said I could go on the road with him and his crew in their RV. But I couldn't make that commitment because I was still in school.

Ten years later, I went to a concert. Bob was up on stage, singing with my favorite band.

By that time, he was famous as (......). He had followed his dreams to major success. I was so glad I'd met him. I'd learned valuable lessons from him.

Eventually I was sent to another school on Long Island. A private school, the campus was only about forty minutes away from where I lived. The school was small but nice. I met a lot of students I liked, including this beautiful girl. Jessie had long, wavy hair with blonde highlights. She had a great smile and an adorable cleft in her chin.

Jessie's best friend Ann was big boned, tough, and very beautiful. The three of us were friends with this cool kid, James. He lived in a nice neighborhood and was friendly with the son of famous guitarist. His dad was one of the most famous guitar players in the world. There were fun parties every weekend at James' estate.

Then there was Andrea. Just being near her made my heart pound, and she knew it. I was too shy at the time to make a move, though. I have always regretted that.

School was good, but there was a kid who made problems for us. We nicknamed him Mr. Troublemaker. He acted like he was your friend, and then ran to the principal to squeal on you. He did this to everyone.

My friend Gary had attended the school years before me. When I told him I was going there, he decided to drop by and visit me.

Gary was still friendly with the principal and vice principal of the school. He spoke with them over coffee. At lunchtime, I saw Gary walking down the hall with the two of them. As they came toward me, all three of them were laughing.

The principal said, "Grant, you never mentioned you were friends with Gary!"

I replied, "I just found out a few days ago he went to this school."

Gary gave me a sly grin.

From that day on, I had fringe benefits; exceptions were made on my behalf. I never got into trouble when Melvin reported on me. Instead, Melvin would get in trouble for ratting me out. He tried reporting me to the vice principal, then the principal. Both turned on him, which made me smile. So did the rest of the kids Mr. Troublemaker had ratted out. He was told to keep his nose out of where it didn't belong.

A year later the school closed. Another closure due to lack of finance.

I was assigned to go to a local school, where I would be tutored along with three other teenagers. On the first day, I arrived early and met my teacher Sarah and her assistant Karen. Sarah was great, but I didn't like Karen. Then the other students arrived. I knew Debbie, she was dating my friend Will. The other girl I didn't know, but she seemed nice. We waited for the third new kid to arrive.

In walked Melvin.

What were the odds? I wished I had that much luck with the lottery.

Melvin smirked at me and I looked at him with disappointment. The kid had a horrible jealous streak in him, and he acted on it with everyone. He enjoyed getting people in trouble because he was always getting in trouble himself.

Sarah was young for a teacher, and she knew I liked her. I guess it was obvious. One day I was the only kid in class. When she asked if I would like to study someplace else, I said, sure, smiling from ear to ear.

We were walking to her minivan when Mr. Troublemaker arrived. He was late to class as usual. He saw us getting into Sarah's van.

Melvin ran inside the school and found Karen in another class. He ratted us out to Karen, telling her there was something developing between Sarah and me.

Karen ran outside to the parking lot. We were in the van deciding where to go. A restaurant, a café, a park with picnic tables? Karen screamed at us. She was freaking out.

She said to Sarah, "If you don't go back to the classroom right now, I will call the police. You'll lose your license to teach after I inform the school board of this incident."

We went back to the classroom.

So I missed out on having a wonderful experience because of that rat kid. He had gotten his revenge on me. And poor Sarah had to suffer because of it.

The good news was I graduated high school with honors.

The bad news was I had twenty-two additional credits, way more than what I needed to graduate. My school files had been badly mismanaged. I could have graduated two years earlier than I did.

CHAPTER 3

THE ART GALLERY

My first job after high school was at Gary's art gallery on Long Island. I started out sweeping floors, and then I moved on to doing sales and inventory. Eventually I became the assistant manager of his multimillion dollar establishment.

The gallery featured a broad range of famous artwork from around the world. Gary was cultured, and his English was perfect. Gary's mother was a history professor and an expert in the English language. Whenever she came to the gallery, she gave me a lesson in proper elocution. They were classy and intelligent people. Gary showed me a different side of life, a much better way to live. Or so I thought.

Some days after work, we went to his place. When it was cold, he lit the fireplace. He showed me how to take three types of gourmet coffee beans, put them in a grinder, and create the most fabulous blend.

After the coffee was ground, Gary would ask if I was hungry. One day I said yes. Then Gary did something unusual.

He grabbed a slab of granite and heated it in the oven. After it was hot, he brought the hot slab to the dinner table and set it on a towel. He then sliced up pieces of chicken, and tossed them onto the hot granite. The chicken began to sizzle, and Gary cooked it until it browned on both sides.

Gary laughed and said, "Now you can tell your friends you ate cooked chicken off a slab of granite."

The dish was delicious. When Gary was good, he was the best.

But when he was bad, he was the devil himself.

One day Gary picked me up at my house because we had an eleven a.m. appointment to hang some artwork. The customer had purchased a painting from the gallery and they wanted us to hang it at their house.

In order to get to the neighborhood where the customer lived, we had to drive over a dam. The dam divided up an estuary, acting as a nursery for both freshwater and saltwater life.

"It was built hundreds of years ago," Gary told me as we drove past. He said, "When the dam floods, it happens around the same time every year. The people who live in this town and in the surrounding towns come here and help save the fish."

"Why do they need to save the fish?" I asked.

"Because when the dam floods, the fish get stranded on the road. They can die if they don't get back in the water fast enough. The act of saving the fish has been a tradition here for a very long time."

I was impressed. "I think that's great. It's the right thing to do."

Gary said, "It's also a way to catch up with neighbors you haven't seen in a while. Everybody has their own life, and they get caught up in their own thing. This is the perfect way for friends to meet up, do something worthwhile, and have some fun."

I agreed.

Our customer's estate was a gorgeous masterpiece. The lawn, the bushes, the entire landscape was perfectly manicured. The owner must have hired a landscape designer to create the exquisite topiary. Everything was lush and green, and the delightful fragrance of blooming flowers traveled through the air note by note. I was entranced.

Inside, we had the choice of taking the stairs or the elevator up to where the painting needed to be hung. It was an easy job, but it needed to be done right. We hung the artwork perfectly.

As we were leaving, I wondered what our client had done for a living. Each one of our customers was quite wealthy and most were interesting people. They were nice so it was a pleasure meeting them. They always made me feel comfortable and accepted. I did my job well, careful to pay attention to details. In the art world, details are everything.

After the job was completed, we headed over to a historical landmark in town, a little stand that sold ices. The small shed was home to a business that had been selling homemade ices for well over a hundred years. I once took my dad there because I loved their chocolate ices. My dad liked lemon ices, but he had never had one at the historic stand. He was so surprised when he found lemon seeds in his cup.

I said, "See, Dad, it really *is* homemade."

He replied, "You're right."

I said, "They don't add the pits to make it *seem* real."

He looked at me for a long moment, then we both laughed.

Gary and I headed to the gallery and worked all day. After we closed up, he drove me home. On the way, we passed more beautiful estates. I watched the shiny horses running, and stared at the cows grazing in the green grass.

Gary stopped at a cider mill. He said, "Let's get some cider, cookies, and apple pie to bring home. For our parents."

I thought it was a great idea. The mill had excellent apple cider, the best I'd ever encountered. Their apple pies were big and juicy, and the cookies were sweet and delicious. After that, we stopped there often on the way home.

Another time Gary drove me home, he stopped in an historic town. The village section was only one block long, another historical landmark. The village itself was over three hundred years old. There was only one restaurant and several stores.

We purchased fresh cashew butter with warm French bread to take home. I also purchased some preserves. I liked a chunky strawberry preserve spread on my toast in the morning. So we stopped there often after that.

Life was good. Then I learned Gary's middle name was trouble With a capital T.

GARY T.

Gary had some friends who I thought seemed kind of shady. He also had this need to steal. He did it not for the money, but for the thrill of it. He was worth millions of dollars. Yet when he could, he would steal hundreds of dollars' worth of caviar and bring it home to his mother.

His mother would say, "Where on earth did you get all this caviar?"

Gary would smile at me and say, "Grant and I just came back from the store."

I would look at him like he was crazy, but he would laugh. He had a roar of a laugh.

Gary took me on vacation to Vermont, where his cousins owned a five-star restaurant and hotel. The endless mountain trails were covered with snow, and the tall pine trees were white and magnificent. The air was crisp, the food was fresh. We ate pancakes with the best maple syrup I'd ever had.

After the weekend ended, it was back to work. We needed to hang some expensive artwork in one of the most exquisite estates I'd ever seen. The place was right out of a fairytale, with rolling acres of lush green land, beautiful flowers everywhere, and an army of butlers and maids who lived in little cottages made of stone. The mansion had an east wing and a west wing, with elevators as an option instead of the adjoining spiral staircases.

As we hung the painting for our customer, I wondered again what the people did for a living. How did someone get that wealthy?

Soon after that, I found out Gary had set me up to be initiated into a private club. He did this without informing me.

I was shocked. I couldn't afford the club, nor did I wish to be a member. I was embarrassed and humiliated when I spoke to the person in charge. "I have no interest in joining, with all due respect," I told the man on the phone.

He was cool about it and the error was immediately corrected.

Why would anyone in their right mind do this to a friend?

After that, Gary must have been forced to endure the consequences of his actions. He seemed angry with me.

Our friendship had been ruined.

I decided to leave the art gallery and find a new job.

Years later I learned, he was moonlighting for an alphabet agency.

He was no good and I'm glad he's out of my world!

CHAPTER 4

A NEW START

I found an apartment in another town and landed a new job at a well known department store in the jewelry department, which added up to a new life. And I met a woman.

Dawn was beautiful with satin skin and great big dimples.

We were happy together, and we fell in love. Everything was cake for nine months.

Then Dawn's ex started coming around, harassing her.

I said, "So why is he harassing you? You guys are divorced, so what's his problem?"

Dawn replied, "I am so sorry, Grant. My divorce will be finalized in a month."

I couldn't believe it. She was still married? I said, "You lied to me!"

Dawn cried while she was apologizing.

I left her apartment after dark. Her husband had been tracking us, like a detective. He knew I was at her apartment. When I walked past, I noticed the unmarked car. He was waiting for me. Watching and waiting.

I called Dawn the next day. "So what does your husband do for a living?"

Dawn's reply was one no guy ever wants to hear. "My soon to be ex-husband is the chief of police."

To make matters worse, he sounded scary big. She told me he was six foot six, rippling with muscles, and the former star of his college football team.

I hung up the phone and did some thinking. I didn't call Dawn for a couple of days.

I was walking down my street and a guy I knew from the old neighborhood approached me. He was a bad guy, not someone I wanted to bump into. He pulled me aside and said, "Call Dawn."

I was surprised. "Tony, you know Dawn?"

"Yeah," he replied. "Her brother is my boss. He manages one of the largest construction companies around. I'm also friends with Dawn's husband."

I went to my doctor, and he gave me a prescription for a sedative. If you had been in my shoes, wouldn't you have needed something to calm *you* down?

I called Dawn but she didn't pick up. I called and called and called. No answer.

Now I was in real trouble. I decided I would move away to the mountains. I began to look into it.

That's when a guy I knew introduced me to Jenny. She was nice, but not my type. I wasn't about to sleep with her anyway. I had enough troubles.

Mort and I had grown up in the same neighborhood. His family struggled more than others and, for this reason, Mort was jealous of everyone on the block. He hated the idea that everybody assumed his family was successful. That really pissed him off.

At some point Mort must have decided to get revenge on the old neighborhood by attempting to curse me with a death sentence.

Jenny and I became friends, even though we weren't sleeping together. One day she told me, "Mort found out through a mutual friend of ours that I'm sick. I'm HIV positive. He paid me one hundred dollars to sleep with you and try to get you infected."

What?

I was infuriated. I thought of all kinds of things I could do to Mort to make him sorry, but I didn't. In fact, I didn't do anything because that would have made me just as sick and demented as he was.

I told Jenny, "Let Mort think I slept with you and that his plan worked."

She agreed to tell him that.

When I saw Mort a few days later, I made believe everything was fine and that I knew nothing about his agenda. We went out for a beer.

As we stood by the bar watching the game on TV, Mort said in a strange voice, "You better enjoy your life, buddy."

I acted surprised and said, "Why?"

Mort shrugged. "No reason. You just better enjoy your life right now."
He said this with a big friendly smile.
After that, I never spoke to Mort again.

CHAPTER 5

THE MOUNTAINS

I found a beautiful cottage nestled in the rolling hills on the side of a gorgeous mountain. About ninety minutes or so from NYC, the location was perfect for me. My new town was far away from where I had been living but, as it turned out, not far enough.

After a few weeks, my new apartment looked great and I was starting to settle in. I searched every day, but work was scarce. I finally landed a job for a limo company.

The limo people were terrific. The owner gave me the coat off his back when he noticed I wasn't dressed warm enough for the winter cold.

The town I lived in was located near Woodstock, the well-known artists' colony. The surroundings were beautiful and quaint. With my new job, I traveled there a lot. I met many interesting artists, some of whom were eccentric, to say the least.

One day there was a private party at a popular restaurant in town that was also a club. The entrance was taped off to the public. I decided to go in anyway. I ducked under the tape and slipped through the side entrance.

When I walked in, a woman smiled at me from across the room. I went over to the bar to talk with her. Her hair was long, and she had a great smile. She said, "Hey, I'm Michelle, can I buy you a beer?"

I replied, "Okay, sure. I'll get the next round."

Michelle and I had the most interesting conversation about music. She was bright and knowledgeable.

I excused myself and went to the restroom. As I was walking back to the bar, a man stopped me. The guy must have been about six foot four, skinny, nice and polite. He said, "Hey, you seem cool. But I know everybody here, and I don't know you. The reason why I say this is because it's *my* party!"

He smiled at me. I thought he was kind of funny so I smiled back.

"What's your name?" he asked.

"Grant," I replied.

He turned to his security guy and asked, "See if there's a Grant on our guest list."

I stood there feeling stupid while the security guard checked the list. After he shook his head, the skinny guy asked me, "So, are you here with someone?"

I said I was and pointed to Michelle. She smiled and held up her beer glass.

He looked at me with disbelief. "You're here with Michelle?"

I nodded.

He told his security guard to keep me there until he got back. Then he went over and asked her if she knew me.

She smiled. "He's my guest. Is there a problem?"

"No, no, everything's cool!"

The guy came back across the room. He said, "Dude, everything's cool! I didn't know you were her guest, man. Enjoy the party! Talk with everyone! Have fun!"

At the time, I didn't know who she was. I didn't realize she was the well-known musician.

And the party's host was (.........) who would go on to become one of the top late night talk show hosts on TV.

MY NEIGHBOR STUART

The guy who lived next door was having all kinds of problems. He wasn't home much, he seemed to be there mostly on the weekends. One day I heard him ranting. He seemed to be hysterical about something.

He stormed out of his apartment and ran to his car. The sky was dark and it was raining. As he rushed out between thunder booms, he dropped something.

Paper flew everywhere in the wet gusts of wind.

Stuart drove off, so I went outside to collect the papers for him. The pages were everywhere, dozens of them scattered all over the ground. I spent an hour collecting page after page from what appeared to have been a diary.

Back inside, I put the pages away in a plastic bag. I stuck the bag in my closet. I had to admit, I was tempted to read it. Somehow I resisted.

Six months went by and there were no signs of Stuart.

One day I was cleaning my closet. I opened the bag and tried to put the pages in some kind of order. But how can you do that without reading everything?

Stuart had led an interesting life.

He had been divorced several times, and he had problems with the government related to taxes. He was also, according to his diary, a person of interest.

His diary stated that his daughter had been abducted. The little girl had disappeared. Supposedly, madmen had kidnapped her and demanded a large ransom. Stuart's ex-wife claimed she knew nothing. She was frantic.

I made a pot of coffee and kept reading. I was hooked.

Stuart's first wife Connie claimed he suffered from a host of mental problems. Over time, she said, Stuart became detached from everything, including her and their daughter. So Connie divorced him.

Stuart's second wife, Elisa, loved Stuart, but after they were married, he changed. According to Elisa, he became aggressive, even violent, and his temper was horrific. He had bursts of anger that seemed to come out of nowhere. Elisa said she confronted Stuart and tried to speak to him, but he hit her in the face and knocked her down. Then, in a strange tone, he asked her, *Are you one of them?*

When she told him she was his wife, Stuart started crying and he held her gently, apologizing. He said, "I'm so sorry, Elisa. I think there's something wrong with me."

The next day, Elisa asked Stuart to find an apartment somewhere else and to get some help because she was filing for divorce. Stuart begged Elisa to give him another chance, but she said she couldn't live with him anymore.

Stuart found an apartment in Poughkeepsie and began working with a psychiatrist there. Dr. Phillips seemed to help him. Since he'd been in therapy, his thinking was clearer and he had more control over his emotions. He met a woman named Tonya, and a year later they decided to get married.

Then there were cutbacks at the company he worked for, and Stuart was laid off. He went home to break the bad news to Tonya. Everything will be all right, Tonya said, just relax.

Stuart scrambled to find a new job at another firm. He went on interview after interview, but weeks passed without any luck.

Stuart got this crazy look in his eyes.

Dr. Phillips had told him to remain busy and productive in order to stay mentally sharp and healthy. But this was not happening for Stuart. In fact, he had become increasingly frantic, and fearful for his own sanity. He overmedicated himself without telling Tonya.

Finally, he found a part-time job in a department store. He and Tonya decided to get married. Tonya was well off and Stuart had some money saved, so after the ceremony they took a cruise to Aruba.

It was beautiful, but Stuart had built up a consistent blood level of meds at twice the proper level. He'd been doubling up on his meds. He went from having a crazy look in his eyes once in a while to looking completely insane.

Tonya didn't know what to do. Certainly, the tequila Stuart was drinking on their honeymoon was not helping the situation.

Stuart became paranoid, suspicious of everyone. He said he felt like everyone was talking about him. With the way he looked, he was probably right. He could hardly sleep, and when he got a little shuteye, the nightmares were too much. He would wake up in a cold sweat.

Stuart and Tonya were divorced soon after they returned to the mainland.

In the midst of a major breakdown, Stuart called Dr. Phillips. The doctor said, "Come to my office immediately. And don't drive."

Stuart jumped in a cab. When he arrived at the doctor's office, he explained how he had been overmedicating himself. Dr. Phillips said, "I need to put you in a facility for an indefinite period of time. We need to evaluate you. We'll get you back in balance."

Stuart admitted himself that same day. He was placed in a little room that overlooked a small lake. The meals were nutritional. Stuart spoke with Dr. Phillips and the other counselors every day while taking his meds in the proper dosages. He still had problems sleeping.

Then the staff that worked the night shift reported something strange. They said he seemed different and spoke in a different manner at night. And first thing in the morning, he acted strange.

The therapists watched him closely. Throughout the day Stuart kept changing. His demeanor, personality, speech patterns, and the way he walked were dramatically different at different times of day and night.

The hospital ran a panel and gave Stuart a battery of tests. The conclusion was Stuart had multiple personalities.

He was not able to keep track of all of the personalities that lived inside his head. He couldn't remember what each of "them" did and said.

This explained the abduction of his daughter. She'd been missing for a while when the authorities picked her up in New York City. She had been staying the whole time at an apartment Stuart rented. Her grandmother had been watching over her, and she was fine.

One of his personalities had brought her there, but Stuart had no recall. He thought she'd been kidnapped.

His mother and daughter had been worried about Stuart. He hadn't explained why he moved them to the apartment. Stuart's mother eventually decided to call Connie, who rushed to the apartment.

Connie got full custody of their daughter after that.

The Feds had been called in when the abduction was first reported. They had been keeping tabs on Stuart ever since.

After reading the whole thing, I left Stuart's diary by his front door. I went out of town for a few days.

When I returned, Stuart had moved out. Another neighbor told me there was a van in the parking lot. A moving crew had moved his stuff out over the weekend.

That was the last I ever heard about Stuart.

CHAPTER 6

WHAT ARE THE ODDS?

I was walking through town one day and ran into Mr. Troublemaker. That's when I realized I hadn't moved far enough away from my old stomping grounds.

Melvin told me he had recently bought a home in town with his fiancée. They wanted to live in the mountains, he said. But the truth was he had moved out of the city due to all the trouble he was in. He'd been mixing chemicals in his basement, and a neighbor had called in the Feds.

I had moved away to someplace beautiful, only to watch it turn ugly right before my eyes. I was one hundred and twenty-five miles away from Long Island. But here was Melvin, standing right in front of me on the sidewalk we apparently shared.

Melvin must have been dreaming up a way to get me in trouble again from that day on. After all, he was Mr. Troublemaker.

Around the same time, I made a new friend. Jack was an interesting guy. He introduced me to some cool people, many who are celebrities that I cannot mention.

Jack invited me to his home many times.

One day while I was at his house having a beer, he went to the bathroom. I noticed a weird box on the table next to the couch. The box was the size of a book of matches.

I couldn't resist checking it out. I picked it up and turned a little dial. A red blinking light went on.

When Jack came back from the bathroom, he panicked. He yelped, "Give me that!"

"What is it?" I asked.

Jack looked angry. "You weren't supposed to see it, man. I left it out by mistake."

"So what is it?" I asked, as I handed it back to him.

"I can't tell you, it's classified."

"Stop kidding around," I said with a snort.

He replied, "I am not who I seem to be, Grant. I can't tell you any more than that. You should go."

I thought he was full of it so I got up to leave. "Whatever. See you around."

Later on, I found out there were federal agents all over town investigating drug trafficking. Dressed like hippies and artists, they were scattered everywhere, watching suspects.

One day a pair of agents approached me. They wanted information on Jack and as it turns out, he's friends with Melvin.

Jack was friends with Melvin? That freaked me out.

I told them I didn't know anything and I wasn't interested in getting involved.

As I walked away, I said, "This is America. I'm entitled to my freedom."

One of the men said in a low, threatening voice, "For the next twenty years, I'm going to make your life a living hell."

The next day I received a call informing me that my grandmother was ill. So I rushed back to the city to find out what was happening.

I was more than happy to get away from Jack, Melvin, and all the Feds dressed like hippies.

MY GRANDMOTHER

My grandma was born in the Bronx in the early 1900s. Her grandmother took care of her while her parents were working. As a young woman, my grandmother had a job at the local coffee shop where everyone in the neighborhood went for coffee, breakfast or lunch. Ben, a very famous actor used to frequent the coffee shop with his friends and they would request my grandmother as their waitress. She said they tipped her generously.

My grandmother was a party girl. She would moonlight at the local speak-easies in Manhattan. She sang and danced on stage, as well as serving drinks to guests. She was a real sparkplug, feisty and always ready to have fun.

She also had some temper. If she didn't like you she would let you know it. Later in life she became a pediatric nurse, and she took on all kinds of difficult cases that needed to be managed. Yet she always found things to laugh about.

She was the most fun during the holidays. My dad would tease her because my grandmother overreacted to everything he said. My dad got a real kick from her reactions and they would both laugh. I found it hilarious to sit there and watch them go at it, insulting each other until the rest of us were crying with laughter.

Life was simple back then, and a lot more fun.

My grandmother had developed a cough and she knew she needed antibiotics. She asked a friend to drive her to the local hospital. When they arrived, she discovered her doctor was no longer working there; he had retired a few weeks prior. The new resident M.D. examined her and gave her a prescription for antibiotics.

She left the hospital and went back to the car with her friend. But before they drove off, two doctors ran out to the parking lot and knocked on the window of the car. Both doctors urged my grandmother to come back in; they wanted to do a twenty-four hour evaluation on her. They claimed it would be a simple overnight monitoring.

My grandmother figured if they thought it was important enough to chase her out to the car, she had better take them up on their advice. So she agreed to go back to the hospital for an overnight evaluation.

This was a grave mistake. She never left the hospital.

She was intubated and put on a ventilator. Her glasses mysteriously vanished, so she couldn't see what the staff was doing. Above her head, taped to the wall, a large yellow sheet of paper had been posted. It stated in big bold letters: "This patient has had a mastectomy, do not administer injections in her right arm." When her right breast was removed, the adjoining lymph nodes were taken out as well. This had reduced her defenses and she had less immunity to infection. Which left her open to opportunist infections.

This is what she contracted while spending the one night in the hospital. Who Okayed This?!

By the time I heard about what was going on, my grandmother's right arm was completely butchered. She was being fed through the stomach. She had become ventilator dependent. And her weight was down to a mere forty-two pounds.

The chief of staff spoke to the other doctors about taking her off the ventilator because she was too weak to be weaned off. They discussed performing a tracheotomy. This was not something my grandmother wanted.

I found the chief of staff impossible to reach. So I called my best friend Hank, a lawyer on Long Island. He said, "I don't ordinarily take on these types of cases, but I will for you."

Hank took all necessary steps to take the hospital to court, and we needed a local process server who knew Brooklyn. I looked in the phone book and started calling. They were all too busy to see me except for one, a family-run business. They'd been in operation for more than forty years in the same building on the same street in Brooklyn.

I went to the office and explained everything. Frank Senior was gracious, warm and hospitable. He knew what I was going through and acted compassionate toward me.

Frank Junior was the process server. Frank Senior had been a lawyer for over thirty years.

Over coffee, I mentioned that my uncle was a lawyer in Brooklyn for forty years. Frank Senior asked his name, so I told him. He lit up, and then laughed. He called his wife into the office and told her, and she laughed too. Frank Junior and the other son Tony ran in to find out what the commotion was about.

Frank Senior explained that my uncle had worked with him for ten years at a well-known insurance agency.

My jaw dropped. Small world. My smile was as wide as the Verrazano Bridge.

Frank Senior asked, "Grant, why doesn't your uncle handle this case for you?"

I replied, "When I spoke with my uncle, he said he wouldn't touch this case with a ten foot pole."

Everyone laughed.

When we went to the hospital, that's when things turned serious again. Frank Junior and I were chased out of the hospital several times for taking pictures of the horrific treatments my grandmother was enduring. But I was finally able to have that meeting with the chief of staff to stop the tracheotomy from being executed.

When I finally sat down across from him, the chief of staff looked familiar. I asked him, "How do you pronounce your last name?"

As he enunciated his last name, I remembered my childhood friend Stew. His name was pronounced the same way.

Stew lived around the block. We often hung out and played Ping-Pong. I had never met his father, but the chief of staff had similar features and the same odd last name.

I said, "I know this is a long shot, but I figure I will ask you anyway."

A busy and impatient man, the chief of staff interrupted me. "What are you getting at, Mr. Davis?"

When I asked if he had a son named Stew, he smiled. Then he got up to close the door to his office, and sat back down. "How do you know my son?"

I told him about our friendship when we were kids, adding, "He mentioned you many times."

"I hope he said some nice things?"

I replied, "Well, you know your son better than I do."

He laughed.

I said, "Stew did say he didn't see you as much as he would've liked to after the separation."

He nodded. "Yes, especially with my job here at the hospital."

"It's a huge responsibility."

He said sadly, "Yes, it really is, Grant." He paused, and then said, "Since there has been a turn of events here, I will hold off on the tracheotomy for as long as possible. We can wait until you get the proper papers in order. I respect the love you have for your grandmother."

I was touched. "She's the only grandmother I have left. So, thank you very much, sir. You are one-of-a-kind."

He smiled and said, "You know you are too, right?"

My grandmother wanted to be taken off the ventilator. She certainly didn't want a tracheotomy performed on her. She was able to scrawl on a piece of paper that she was of sound mind and would rather die than be tortured any longer.

The hospital psychiatrist evaluated her mental condition. He explained to her in detail that if they stopped treating her, she would die.

She wrote, "I will take my chances."

Within a few days after being taken off the ventilator, my grandmother passed away. I was heartbroken. My crying went on for days. The grief lingered for weeks.

My pain stemmed from seeing the barbaric tactics used on my poor grandmother. Her treatment in the hospital made me feel mentally injured. And the result was she died too soon.

MY DAY IN COURT

The Feds who had approached me about Jack were still in my life. They seemed to be keeping an eye on me, hoping I would agree to work with them. So when my case against the hospital went to court, they asked the judge if they could be present at the proceedings.

In the courthouse both parties had assigned seating. On one side sat the hospital lawyers and doctors. When the Feds sat down, every seat was taken. On my side, there was only my lawyer, my aunt, and me. I was clearly outnumbered.

When it was time for me to take the stand, someone shouted out, "Lock him up and throw away the key!"

The judge looked up. "Who said that? I will not tolerate these types of disturbances in my courtroom."

As the court trial went on, my grief overwhelmed me. I took time out to gather myself in the men's room. As I huddled in the bathroom stall, I began crying. I was looking at the photos of my grandmother, the ones I had been chased out of the hospital for taking. I was not allowed to submit them to the judge, they were considered inadmissible. This was so unfair!

A court custodian came into the restroom. He heard me and tried to be comforting. I showed him the pictures of my grandmother I wasn't allowed to submit. He thought this was unfair too.

He took a few of the photos and put them in his pocket while I cleaned up. Then he went to speak to the judge.

In control of my emotions again, I returned to the courtroom.

When I went up on the stand to testify, one of the Feds yelled out, "Hang him with a noose!"

The judge told the stenographer to stop typing. He stared at the Feds. "Your higher ups asked me to allow you in my courtroom during this trial. Need I remind you this is a federal courthouse? You may be federal agents on the outside, but inside this courtroom you are in my domain and I trump your authority. I'm making a note to myself to contact your superiors, to explain to them how you disrupted and disrespected a higher authority. I'm also holding you both in contempt of court for the sum of ten thousand dollars."

The Feds were escorted out of the courtroom.

The judge then looked at the pictures the custodian had handed him privately. He flipped through the photos with great disgust, and then looked up at the defense. "My god, this is pure butchery! This poor lady has been tortured."

The defense lawyer said, "Those pictures can't be submitted! The pictures we agreed upon have already been submitted."

The judge looked at her and said, "Well, that's too bad because I'm going to make an exception."

The judge then asked me how I knew the process server. I replied, "I found them in the phone book, but they knew my uncle, a lawyer on Court Street in downtown Brooklyn."

The judge asked who my uncle was, so I told him. He smiled. "So why didn't you have him handle this situation for you?"

I replied, "He's semi-retired, and he told me he wouldn't touch this case with a ten foot pole."

The judge laughed and winked at me.

We won the case.

The hospital lawyers immediately started questioning the judge's decision making. The judge got angry, his face red, his voice loud. "Are you questioning my authority and my ability to make decisions because you lost this case? Because, if I thought for a second you were, I would have you disbarred!"

My grandmother had no rights while she was in the hospital. My case changed this. My case was one of many stories and legal actions that helped to secure the passing of The Patient's Bill of Rights.

These days, patients have more of a say in the medical treatments they receive.

THE FEDS

The Feds had promised me the next twenty years of my life were going to be a living hell. Now they would make sure that this was indeed the case.

When I arrived back upstate at my country retreat, I was told that some men had been in my apartment going through my things. The chief of police was not on my side so I could not call upon him for help. After all, I had flirted with his wife.

Of course, I was unaware she was still his wife at the time. He had made that clear when he came to see me. He also let me know the Feds were watching me, and it would be a good idea for me not to talk with his ex.

I replied "Roger that!"

A few weeks later there was another break-in at my apartment. Two men forced their way in. They held me down and injected me with something. I figured it was a biological agent of some kind. The word mycoplasma a word I never heard of stayed etched in my memory.

I was sick for several weeks. When I felt better, I made my way into town to pick up some food.

Jack and his friends approached me and apologized about the break-ins. They said there was nothing they could do about the Feds; it was out of their hands. But Jack knew the guy who was responsible for the agent used in the injection, and he agreed to introduce us.

I was introduced to the provider of the biological agent, a geeky guy in high-top sneakers. I asked him what I had been injected with.

He said, "It's classified, but if you don't take care of yourself, you're going to be very sick. This could take weeks, months, possibly years. But when the agent becomes active within you, it will attack with a vengeance. It is very aggressive. Monitor yourself regularly, you really have to stay on top of this monster," he said with a frown.

Who Okayed This?!

I had a series of blood tests done, and various other lab tests. When the blood work came back, everything was normal. I did not have hepatitis A, or B, but the hep C results were indeterminate. This concerned me, so I had the test redone. The lab reported the same results.

Now I was nervous. When I called the lab to find out the status of my HIV results, the head of the lab got on the phone. He said, "Mr. Davis, I have personally reviewed your lab results because my lab technicians ran into a brick wall trying to figure out what on god's green earth they were looking at."

My heart raced. I said, "Sir, what exactly are you telling me?"

He replied, "I have lanced a lot of fingers and I have drawn plenty of blood, studying all forms of microscopic life forms from bacteria to every type of virus imaginable. But Mr. Davis, I have never in all my years seen anything like what I saw in your blood."

I was speechless.

"You don't have HIV, but you have something that nobody here has ever seen before."

Terrific. Now what? "So what do I do?"

He said, "I suggest we wait a few weeks and redo the test. That's all I can suggest, aside from going to the CDC to see if they can help you determine what's going on."

Now I was really scared. What kind of world was this in which the people that are supposed to protect you infect you instead? It was not a free world that much was true. When there are gray subdivisions of certain government agencies, coupled with rogue agents out on the prowl, the free world was nothing but a myth. Who could you trust?

My answer was to trust no one.

The day before I left town, I passed by some hippies sitting on a park bench in the town square. One of them stood up, pointed at me, and yelled out, "There he goes, the one that got away!"

CHAPTER 7

BACK TO LONG ISLAND

I moved back to Long Island and settled in to live with my parents. Even though July was hot, it was nice to be back in my hometown.

My dad and mom were thrilled to see me. My father was especially happy to meet Scotty, the dog I had adopted. My dad was used to big dogs, not a little pug with a Napoleon complex. Scotty was the most caring dog. He always drew a lot of attention, and he loved to prance around like a miniature Clydesdale.

My dad and Scotty bonded right away. My dad would come home from work and say, "Where is that little runt?" Scotty would run to him, do circles around my dad, then run away. Then he would run back, wrestle with my dad, and lick his chin. They were quite the pair.

My dad grew so attached to Scotty; he could not fall asleep without the dog nestled under his arm.

A few months later, my dad began to have problems urinating. He had to drive himself to the hospital in the middle of the night to get catheterized. The doctors taught him how to do it for himself at home.

A few days later he was driving home from work listening to the radio and he heard a commercial for an experimental machine that could shrink an enlarged prostate. He wrote down the phone number to call for free information about the procedure.

After receiving a brochure in the mail and going over all the information, he made an appointment. The office was about an hour away from where we lived, so I drove him there.

The machine the doctors were using would shrink the prostate by way of microwave radiation, and the patient needed to be grounded by having a steel rod inserted through the rectum. This didn't sound like a good idea to me, but my dad wanted to go ahead with it.

After the first treatment my dad was able to urinate without having to self-catheterize. After the second treatment it became even easier. After the third treatment, however, he didn't feel well. As we drove home, he told me he was feeling faint. I took him to the hospital.

He received an immediate blood transfusion. After that, my dad's health went spiraling downhill.

My mother called me from work and said I should rush over to the hospital to see my dad. When I arrived, I ran to my dad's room. He took one look at me and said, "Oh shit, if you're visiting me here, that means I must be finished! Grant, please leave the room for a few minutes."

I stood outside his room and, for the second time in my life, heard my dad crying his eyes out.

After about twenty minutes, I walked back into my dad's room. He said, "I didn't want you to have to see me like this, but I'm so upset!"

I asked the nurse caring for my dad where the doctors were. She said they were over in the west wing. She showed me the phone to use to track down my dad's primary physician.

I was in the east wing dialing the west wing. How insane. The operator paged the doctor for me. I waited and waited. Finally he answered the phone.

I said, "Hello, Dr. Smith, what is the status report on Mr. Davis?"

He asked, "Who is this?"

I replied, "Grant."

Dr. Smith said, "Grant, Mr. Davis had a blood transfusion that we suspect might've been tainted with Hep C, HIV, or both."

What?

I said, "How can such a thing happen to people here?"

He snorted. "Dr. Grant, we are both doctors so we both know these things happen every day. You should be used to this by now. You know how the system works. Anyway, where did you do your residency? I haven't heard your name mentioned before."

I replied, "Dr. Smith, I didn't do my residency for the simple reason I'm not a doctor and the patient Mr. Davis is my father."

Dr. Smith slammed the phone down. Probably he was afraid he would lose his license…to kill.

My dad preferred to die in his own home. We set up a hospital bed in the living room with all the medical equipment needed. Within two days my father had passed away.

But this was after my dad had to suffer a horrific, tormented death.

As I looked at my father, his thin body lifeless on the hospital bed, a caseworker from the local hospice pulled me aside. He asked to speak to me in private.

We ducked into the hall. The man was extremely tall and dark, strange looking. He showed me a vial filled with a clear liquid.

"Your father should have been given this remedy, it would have saved his life and none of this would have happened. The product is not sold here in the US. If your father had taken this, none of his suffering would have occurred and he would still be here with you right now."

He smiled and said, "Oh well," then slipped the vial back in his pocket. He gave me an odd look and walked off.

It took all the willpower I could muster not to run after him. I wanted to punch this guy's lights out and shove all his teeth down his throat. My father was dead! How could I ever repeat what this asshole had said to me, to my poor mother? I was pissed off beyond belief.

I wondered if it was a cruel, cold hearted, distasteful joke perpetrated by the Feds. I had no way of knowing.

The unfortunate truth about the untimely deaths of my grandmother and my father is that they have something in common. Once you are over the age of sixty-five, collecting social security and not producing enough income tax, you are expendable. You become useless to the machine. This leads to hospital errors, wrongful deaths, and other preventable tragedies.

THE OLD NEIGHBORHOOD

I was surprised to find out Mort was still living with his mother down the block from me. I was hoping something tragic had happened to him. A neighbor told me Mort had been parking his car twenty blocks away, in another neighborhood. The people there were becoming suspicious.

"Good," I replied. "Maybe somebody there will do a job on him."

My neighbor said, "I thought you guys were friends?"

I replied, "With friends like him, who needs enemies?"

My mother was grieving. She also had financial issues. So she put our house on the market.

Evan, a friend of the family who owned a juice bar in town, invited me to his place. He wanted to cheer me up. Evan, a great guy who could always make me laugh, was supportive of my family.

Evan was freakishly strong. He was a professional fighter, and very protective of me. I should've told him to kick the living shit out of Mort, but I didn't.

Evan was crazy, but he couldn't do enough for me during my time of grievance. He took me out to eat with his fiancé and his friends. We went out to the clubs, where he introduced me to girls. He told everyone the story about how one night he had to sneak past security at the hospital to deliver the fresh juice he had made for my dad.

Evan's girlfriend was very pretty. Somehow Esther had the strength and patience to put up with Evan's crazy antics. She owned a big beautiful place on Long Island, an old house with a rustic feel. She also had two wonderful boys from a previous marriage.

Evan's mom was a fabulous cook. One night she made me the most wonderful spanakopita. It was hot out of the oven, the filo light and flaky, and whatever she added to the spinach was an absolute delight for my taste buds.

Evan's dad was nice, very polite. Evan always behaved well in his presence. Evan's sister Stacy was brilliant. She had a key position in a large firm which eventually relocated her to Switzerland. Evan told me she loved it there. I wondered what it would be like to travel to Switzerland, to explore the Alps.

Great neighbors made for a great neighborhood. I didn't want to sell the house and leave them behind. But we had no choice.

CHAPTER 8

THE HOUSE IS SOLD

We finally closed on the house. My mother had a condo we could live in down in the sunshine state. So we packed up for Florida.

The rental car was filled to the max. The back seat was so full of our belongings; there wasn't much room for poor Scotty.

We had a late start after finalizing all the paperwork for the closing, so we decided to stay at a nearby hotel. I was exhausted and needed a good night's sleep before we set out on the long drive south.

After breakfast, I walked Scotty. Then we were ready to start our road trip.

When we got on I-95, it began to snow. I realized I was headed north instead of south! I turned around and caught the interstate southbound.

The driving was bad. The storm was following us from behind. I wanted to beat the storm because I didn't like driving on ice and snow. The weather remained cold and icy all day.

When we reached North Carolina, we got off the interstate to find a place to stay the night. We drove past a long line of hotels. Most were booked solid because it was holiday time. Thanksgiving was just couple of days away.

We found a nice hotel but we had to sneak in the dog because they didn't allow pets. We took him up the fire escape, a metal staircase in back by the exit door. It was challenging because the stairs had frozen over and it was slippery.

The room was a haven. It was nice to be off the road somewhere warm, out of that cold, gray, gloomy evening.

The next day we were on the road again. South Carolina seemed to go on forever. Then we were in Georgia. The sun was out so we rolled the windows down. After few hours, we reached Jacksonville, Florida.

As we continued south, we passed some orange groves that smelled wonderful. The scent was similar to gardenias. The sweet fragrance was everywhere. It made Scotty stand up and stick his head out the window. I could see him in the rearview, sniffing away. He looked at me in an excited fashion, as if to say, *This must be our new home, I've got to investigate!*

Near Orlando we stopped for some fast food. Not the best food, but much appreciated in a pinch.

After lunch and a good stretch, we continued heading south until we reached Palm Beach County. My mom owned a one bedroom condo she had rented out for many seasons. A good investment and now our home.

When we opened the door, it was one hundred and eight degrees inside. The air conditioner was broken.

We got back in the car and went to a hotel that allowed pets. The desk clerk was nice enough to bump us up to a suite. There was a great restaurant downstairs so we ordered room service. Because Scotty was family and families ate together.

We wound up staying in the hotel for two weeks while we waited for the air conditioner to be repaired. Scotty acclimated quickly. He trotted up and down the halls as if he were the hotel manager and knew exactly which room we were staying in.

Once we had air conditioning, we unloaded the car and put everything away in the now full to the brim condo. My bed arrived, along with everything else we had shipped from home. The place was packed.

My parents' best friends had lived in Florida for forty-plus years. They had promised us they would show us around, but instead decided to travel the world. We were on our own.

We took drives along the beach and learned our way around town. I figured as long as I knew which way was north, south, east, and west, we couldn't get lost. But we did anyway. Finding our way around was fun. How else do you learn about a new place? You have to jump in head first.

My dad never wanted to live in the condo. He considered it solely a source of income. My mother had simple tastes, small was fine with her. She liked the condominium community. There were a lot of activities for people her age.

After a month or so of staying with my mom and enjoying the warm air, the sunshine, the palm trees and ocean breezes, I was captivated by the place.

Then I received a phone call.

A voice said, "We know where you're living."

I replied, "Great! That makes two of us," and hung up.

I was searching for work but I'd had no luck. I needed a job. I needed a purpose, income, and friends.

My mother was happy in Florida but I wasn't. So, once she knew her way around, I moved back to New York. I had decided to live with my aunt for a while.

CHAPTER 9

QUEENS

My Aunt Annie's house was a natural wonder. It was located in Forest Hills, Queens, on preserved land. You could not sit down in her house. It was full of plants and clowns.

Annie was an amazing person. She had red hair, lots of freckles, and looked like Raggedy Ann. She had grown up on the south shore of Long Island. She was one of the nicest, most generous people you could ever meet. But, you did not want to get on her bad side.

On her side of the family, mental illness was prevalent. Annie had severe obsessive compulsive disorder.

For some reason, she had decided everything in her home needed to be catty-cornered. The chairs, the couches, the loveseat, the footstools, the dresser. Even all the food in the refrigerator was catty-cornered.

Aunt Annie loved orchids, all types. She grew species ranging from Cattleya to Lady Slippers. Her lovely orchids covered all the tables in her home including the kitchen table, the coffee table, end tables and night tables. Her windowsills were draped with other plants, and in her sunroom she had a banana tree.

You could only sit down on the bar stools and the beds. Annie, an avid seamstress, had a large collection of clowns. These handmade clowns were three feet tall and she'd seated them on all the chairs and couches in her home. In fact, the clowns seemed to have the run of the house. To make matters even stranger, all of the clowns looked like her.

While I lived with my aunt, I went to a local deli every morning. They made a good breakfast, and the portions were generous. Craig worked behind the counter, and I became friendly with him. I could picture him working in an expensive restaurant because he had good manners and spoke perfect English.

One day he told me that the deli job was part-time and he moonlighted by driving celebrities around for a local limo company.

I was impressed. What a fun job. I said, "That sounds great!"

Craig nodded, and then said, "Nick, my boss, is the best. I'll see if I can get you a job if you're interested."

I replied, "Yes, definitely!"

A few days later Nick called. I went to the limo company office to meet him. Nick was nice, he seemed genuine, honest and sincere. I liked him right away and I understood why celebrities preferred him to drive them around. Nick liked me, too, and he hired me on the spot.

That night I drove the famous opera singer named Peter to an award ceremony. After the engagement, the twenty-one passenger limo was filled with Broadway and movie stars. I drove them to a famous night club on the lower west side.

One of the celebrity guests came out of the club. I recognized her at once.

It wasn't that late, but she said she was tired. She asked me, "Would it be all right if I lie down in the limo for a while and relax?"

I replied, "Of course, ma'am."

She asked my name, then said, "Where's Nick?"

"He had an important engagement to attend, so I'm filling in for him this evening."

"That's fine, you seem very nice," she said.

About an hour later, everyone packed into the limo. I drove them all back to their hotels.

My tip that evening was big. The night had been exciting. And I'd met some amazing people.

Nick called to inform me I'd done a great job. He said he would call whenever he needed me to fill in.

I looked for fulltime work every day. I went on foot to some of the finest jewelry stores in New York. None wanted to hire me.

One day I sat on a bench in Central Park. I took off my shoes and sighed. My feet were blistered and sore. I wished I had brought sneakers to change into.

I put my shoes back on and bit my lip. I needed a break and some food.

JEWEL OF THE CITY

I went to a luncheonette for soup and a sandwich. The soup of the day was cream of tomato. This place was famous for their burgers, so I had a cheeseburger medium-rare with everything on it.

The burger joint was decorated in mahogany, the same décor they'd had for over fifty years. When you entered, you felt like you'd been transported back in time. You could observe the chefs cooking, wearing their big white hats. The prices were old-fashioned too, and affordable.

The soup was delicious, my cheeseburger juicy and amazing. I thought they might be the last place in the city that still knew how to make a perfect egg cream and a great float.

As I ate, I was thinking about all the places I had applied with no definitive answer for my state of unemployment. I decided to give my resume to the finest store on the planet. Why not? After all, sometimes old and well-known shops were the best places to be.

I walked over to this beautiful store. The store windows were tastefully designed, colorful and stylish, created with insight and imagination. People were stopping to stare with astonishment and appreciation.

I took a deep breath and walked inside. The interior was posh, and fabulously decorated. Flowers, vases, abstract designs, fashion jewelry, fine jewelry, clothing from around the world. My eyes feasted on the beauty created by the world's most famous designers.

I went to the human resources department and handed in my resume. As I started to walk away, a beautiful woman with a waterfall of auburn hair stopped me. She said, "Do you have a moment? Human resources would like to spend some time talking with you."

"Certainly, that would be wonderful," I replied with a smile.

I was interviewed by three managers.

Finally, the last manager said, "Grant, do you have time today to meet with the head trainer?"

"Of course," I said.

We took the elevator up to the training floor. When we entered Mr. David's office, he stood up and introduced himself. He turned to the manager and said, "He's perfect!"

The manager turned to me and said, "You're hired, Grant. Training starts next week."

What luck! I was smiling when I shook his hand. I had a job!

Training began the following Monday. Mr. David was intelligent, well spoken, and an impeccable dresser. His mannerisms reminded me of a famous writer. I admired his style and was grateful when he took me under his wing and shined me up like a rough diamond. He was extremely compassionate and considerate, which made me relaxed and comfortable in his presence.

The first week of training was fabulous. My second week of training was even better. Mr. David was thorough, clear, and fun, the best combination for a wonderful learning experience.

Day one on the selling floor took some getting used to, though. Fortunately, I was seasoned from my previous experience and well trained by Mr. David. So the work flowed naturally.

At this store, the clientele were well-known celebrities, politicians, and public figures. I worked with some of the most interesting people one could ever hope to meet. I loved the job so much I usually didn't want to go home at the end of the day. I felt like I was finally home, where I belonged, where I fit in. Working there, I felt alive.

The store itself was the crème de la crème of New York. Shopping here made women feel beautiful, able to fully express their femininity. The store provided access to luxurious accessories from around the world. It was a place where elegance and self-expression could embrace everyone, clientele as well as employees. I was in heaven.

CHAPTER 10

EUROPE

After working many long hours for months, I felt like my health was beginning to deteriorate. My immune system had weakened and I got sick a lot. I was going in downward spiral, so I took a leave from my job to get well again.

I had been injected with a biological agent. I still didn't know what it was. I decided to see what I could find out from a friend who had lived with a serious disease for a long time.

Andy was a world-renowned hypnotist. I had met him years before. Andy and his wife were compassionate people, and we became good friends. Andy looked like a famous dancer.

In my mind, I could picture Andy smiling, umbrella in hand, jumping up and clicking his heels while singing in the rain.

His office was at his home in Queens, in the basement. He held seminars in the living room and sometimes rented space in a learning center in the city. He had lots of students.

Years before, Andy had been diagnosed with a fatal disease. Yet he was still alive and well and very busy.

I went to see him. His home was a nice old house directly across the street from a tremendous graveyard. After he invited me in and we caught up on our lives, I asked how he had treated his illness so successfully. Was there a doctor I could consult, a medication I might take?

He said, "Grant, I tried all the mainstream therapies. Those did absolutely nothing but make me sicker. All I wanted to do was die."

Andy said he had friends in Europe, which was where he was from. They advised him on how his disease would be treated in Europe.

We were sitting on a couple of couches in the basement. Andy looked as pale as a ghost. He told me to watch him as he self-administered a treatment, so I did. He told me he would take some of the formula (he called it that, *the formula*) and I would be able to see how quickly it revived and refreshed him.

He mixed some of the formula into a glass of water, then drank it down. He closed his eyes and, as I watched, all the color returned to his face. He opened his eyes and I noticed they were exceptionally clear. When he smiled, I could see that his energy had returned.

I wanted to try whatever it was Andy was taking, so I asked for his help. He said I would need to find out exactly what would work for my case. So he put me in contact with a man named Stan, a scientist he said would be able to help me. Stan was in town from Germany for a few days so my timing had been perfect.

A couple days later I went to the timeshare where Stan was staying. The condo was full of equipment. He said he had brought it all with him from Germany.

Stan ran all types of tests on me. The testing took four and a half hours.

He printed out an analysis and we sat down together in the living room to go over all the results. Stan shook his head. Then he advised me to go to Bavaria and get treatment for my immune system immediately.

Stan was from the US, but he had elected to study medicine in Switzerland and Germany. He described for me the foothills of the Black Forest, the Swiss Alps, and a tremendous waterfall one could only see by traveling on foot. Stan loved to hike, he was an avid outdoorsmen. He advised me where to go while I was in Europe, as well as guiding me to the right people and the right type of help for my medical needs.

The next day, I purchased an airline ticket to Germany.

The flight was long and uneventful.

When I arrived, I took a shuttle to the resort where I had booked a room. I was stunned by the natural beauty of the area. The countryside was gorgeous, the mountains vast, the foliage immense and green. The air was cold, fresh and crisp. And the people were warm and courteous.

When I arrived at the resort, my bags were taken up fifteen floors to my room. The view was spectacular, I could see people skiing and riding the lifts. The Alps were breathtaking.

I had dinner that evening in a five-star restaurant on the top floor of the hotel. There were crystal chandeliers, with gold leaf trim everywhere. The carpet was burgundy, thick and plush. I had the finest service and the most delicious German food I'd ever eaten.

The next morning, I enjoyed a hot breakfast, then a Swedish massage. My masseuse was pale blonde, beautiful, and very strong. She started on my neck and moved down my back, working through all the nooks and crannies, undoing all the knots. I melted under her hands as she applied generous amounts of warm, almond scented oil.

I was fully relaxed. This was good because, after the massage, I had an appointment to see my new doctor.

THE DOCTOR

I rode a bus to the Black Forest. From there, I called a car service to take me to a very small town deep in the woods.

Dr. Siegfried had arranged to meet me at the local coffee shop. I arrived first and sat down. The shop was old and rustic. I loved the style. It was as if I had stepped back in time hundred years. An antique cuckoo clock chimed and the little bird popped out. So charming.

The doctor arrived, brushing snow off the sleeves of his jacket and shaking out his hat as he hung them on the coat rack.

After we had introduced ourselves, I explained my condition. At the end of our conversation, he agreed to try to help me with my unfortunate health condition. He told me to come to his laboratory the next morning.

The next day, the car service took me to the doctor's office. We went up winding mountain roads, passing white horses running through open fields. When we arrived at the address the doctor had given me, I was pleased to see it was not an office building but an estate.

I got out of the car. The house was huge, set comfortably on acres of wooded land. Horses ran through the snow. The scenario was surreal, like a painting.

I paid my driver and told him I would call him when I was ready to be picked up.

I walked over a footbridge to the doctor's front door. Under the footbridge, a babbling brook connected to a distant river.

The door knocker was old, it looked ancient. The doctor greeted me and invited me inside.

The ceilings were high, the décor old-fashioned Bavarian. Oil paintings covered the wallpapered walls. A fire roared in a huge fireplace.

The doctor said, "Come sit down here, near the fireplace. You can warm up and relax. I'll be with you in a few moments. Would you like some hot cocoa?"

I said sure.

The butler walked over to me a few minutes later. "Here, sir, is your cocoa. Please be careful, it's very hot."

I thanked him graciously.

So, there I was, sitting on a chair that resembled a king's throne, in front of an enormous fireplace, with the most delicious cup of hot cocoa I'd ever tasted. And I was there waiting to speak with Dr. Siegfried, the only person I had found who said he might be able to help me get well.

Dr. Siegfried was a zoologist as well as a world-renowned physicist.

As I listen to the crackling fire, Dr. Siegfried came back and sat down. "Are you feeling a bit more relaxed now?"

I smiled and said, "Yes. It would be impossible *not* to feel peaceful and at ease in these beautiful surroundings."

Dr. Siegfried invited me to follow him to the lab. We walked to the west wing of his estate, to his private laboratory.

The lab was large and clean. A blackboard covered with quadratic equations stood by the windows. I looked around at the oscilloscopes and microscopes, the beakers and vials filled with stuff. There was all sorts of equipment, and a bunch of generators.

We sat down together on stools. He asked me how I thought I had contracted my debilitating fatigue and poor immunity.

I hadn't wanted to go into it, but he was my doctor. So I told him I had been injected with some type of infectious agent.

He looked startled. He asked, "Who would do this to you?"

I looked into his wise eyes. He didn't need to know the details. It might not be safe for him to hear about my personal troubles. So I said, "It's complicated, but this is what happened to me and now I need your help."

Dr. Siegfried said, "I see." Then he put his glasses on. "Let's get right to work. Would you roll up your sleeve for me? I want to take a sample of your blood and do an analysis."

I complied and he drew blood from my arm, then lanced my finger and my ear.

He collected the blood, put it on a slide, and slid it under a microscope connected to a television.

While he was examining the slide under the microscope, he asked, "Have you ever had dark field microscopy performed on you?"

"No, I don't think so."

He indicated that I should look carefully at the screen to study the slide of my blood. "Look here, Grant, see this organism? Well, it is foreign to the human blood. Do you see what it's doing? This creature is mimicking your white blood cells, then sabotaging them slowly. Your immune system thinks this organism is a part of the system." He paused, then said in a low voice, "What you have inside you is bioengineered. It creates a vacuum for other infectious diseases to take hold of your cellular biology."

I sat up straight, frightened by this revelation.

He continued. "I would like to test, in vitro, then in vivo, to see what works on this organism. To stop it in its tracks. But I will need to see the results of your complete blood count first. So let's go upstairs and have lunch while it's being prepared and analyzed by my assistant."

Still in shock, I stood up. My legs were weak and shaky.

We left the lab and walked down a long carpeted hallway. On the way, I admired the impressionist artwork he had on the walls, as well as the bronze statues and antiques.

We reached a dining room and Dr. Siegfried said, "Sit wherever you'd like. Angus will be with us shortly."

Some dark bread had been prepared, and tea was set out on the table. The dishes, utensils, and teapot were silver.

I asked the doctor, "Who's Angus?"

"My chef. Angus has been with us many, many years. Right now he's preparing our lunch. I hope you like duck?"

The view from the large picture windows was remarkable. It was beginning to snow. The doctor looked at me, his face kind. He asked, "Do you like snow?"

"I like to watch it as it falls from the sky, as it collects on the trees and the road," I replied.

"Are you a skier?"

"I have skied before, but with my condition, everything takes a lot of effort."

"I understand. Well, let's see if we can make you feel better."

"That would really be wonderful," I said.

Angus had a beautiful assistant named Ursula. She helped serve a roasted duck from the northern side of the forest, complete with all the garnishing. The soup of the day was cream of leak with smoked chicken, and this was served with potato that was twice baked, with a dollop of sour cream and chives on top.

While we were eating, Dr. Siegfried asked, "Grant did someone you know recommend my therapy?"

I replied, "I found out your treatments existed by observing how well they worked on a friend. He sent me to Stan."

Dr. Siegfried replied, "I see. So you met my former apprentice. Stan was difficult, although we did do some good research. Eventually I had to ask him to leave. He seemed to be picking my brain."

"Did you know Stan's sister is a very well-known actress?" I asked.

"I did not know that. What might I have seen her in?"

I listed some film she had starred in and he smiled. "How interesting. I never knew this about Stan. In fact, he never mentioned he had a sister."

CHAPTER 11

THERAPY

The next morning after breakfast, Dr. Siegfried and I went back to the laboratory. He wanted to share the results of my blood work.

As soon as we sat down, he stated, "Your infection is serious, as you can see by looking at your white blood cell count. We need to get to work on this immediately."

He led me to a corner where a huge machine stood. The front was covered with dials. He told me to sit down and take off my shoes and socks, then he put a wet towel over my bare feet. He gave me two copper cylinders to hold; they were connected to the machine.

"You're going to feel a jolt of electricity, Grant. This is going to happen every thirty seconds for approximately fifteen minutes." He patted my shoulder and said, "I'm setting it on low; gradually we will turn up the dial."

"You're electrocuting me?"

"No," he soothed. "I'm revitalizing your body, and electrocuting the unwanted organisms in your blood simultaneously."

Dr. Siegfried turned the machine on and it buzzed loudly.

Zap!

I felt a little sting. "That's not so bad," I said.

He smiled. "Good! So let's turn it up until we reach your threshold of tolerance."

As he turned up the dial, I responded to the jolts. Finally I had reached my limit. "Okay, okay I think that's as high as you should go."

He said, "Fine. Now this is the proper level for your bioelectric therapy. We'll continue it for the next fifteen minutes."

Zap...zap....zap...

A timer went off with a ringing sound, and a cuckoo bird popped out. As if the timer was an old cuckoo clock. I was starting to think *I* was cuckoo for letting Dr. Siegfried do this to me.

Then he asked how I felt.

I realized I felt immensely better. "Strangely, I feel really good!" I replied.

"Great!" he said. "In a few minutes, I want to try something else."

He wheeled over another machine. "This took me quite a number of years to develop. It's the culmination of my life's work."

"What is it?" I asked.

"I was able to measure the healthy metabolism, record it, then replicate the biological information. I've done this with the human immune system as well."

"What can you do with this information?" I asked.

"My boy, I will show you," Dr. Siegfried said. He then proceeded to place a different set of copper rods in my hands. "The information is going to go within your cells to make you healthy and whole once more."

This was hard for me to believe, but I was desperate and willing to try anything.

Dr. Siegfried turned on the machine and said, "Just sit back and relax. I'll be back in twenty minutes to check on you."

I sat there looking out the window as deer walked about in the snow at the edge of the forest. I forgot about the rods in my hands, the machine doing whatever it was doing to me. The world I was in was incredibly beautiful.

I closed my eyes and took a deep breath, and before I knew it, the twenty minutes was up.

Dr. Siegfried asked, "Grant, how do you feel?"

I mumbled, "Verrrrry relaxed."

"Good," he said. "Within the next few days, you're going to see some remarkable changes in how you feel."

"I hope so," I replied.

When Dr. Siegfried insisted I stay at the estate while I recovered my full health, I agreed to be his guest. Why not? I canceled my room at the resort.

The butler led me to the guest quarters and I lay down on a big soft bed. I had the most peaceful, most colorful dreams.

When I woke up, I looked at the clock. I had been sleeping for only a few minutes, yet it felt like I'd had many hours of deep sleep.

I stood up and walked to the window.

There were children outside playing in the snow on red sleds. They were laughing and having fun, which made me smile.

I walked to the dresser to look at myself in the mirror. I looked different. I was already starting to look better.

A feeling of well-being had come over me, something I had not felt in years.

I left my quarters in search of Dr. Siegfried. I found him relaxing, smoking his pipe in front of the fireplace.

I sat down beside him, and said, "Dr. Siegfried, I'm feeling very good. I have not felt this good in years."

He looked at me, his eyes bright. "Already, your body is reacting positively to the therapies. It is beginning to revive you and enliven the essence of your very being."

"That's exactly how I'm feeling. A deep inner and allover peacefulness."

He said, "Isn't it wonderful? So let's go make our own hot cocoa."

Dr. Siegfried had a jar of the finest cocoa from Belgium, which he blended with fresh milk from his own cows. He heated the milk on an old wood burning stove, explaining that his grandfather had built it over a century ago. When it was ready, once again I was treated to the best hot cocoa I had ever tasted.

When I told this to Dr. Siegfried, he said, "In my home, everyone is treated like a family member."

I said, "Thank you, that's very kind of you. I appreciate your hospitality, your generosity, and your help. More than words can express."

Dr. Siegfried said, "Now I have something else you might like. I happen to know Ursula has her eye on you, Grant."

Dr. Siegfried winked and told me she lived in the cottage west of the footbridge.

I felt so good I decided to pay her a visit.

I went back to my room and got ready, then I put on my coat, scarf, and hat. I walked outside and headed toward the cottage.

"Grant, Grant! Over here!"

Ursula wore a beautiful white jacket, the hood pulled up over her head. This made her sparkling blue eyes even more striking. She had on white gloves and snow boots. She looked like a pretty snow princess.

The expression in her lovely face was warm and sincere. I found that very charming. I liked her, or was I was just falling under her spell?

Ursula said, "As the pastry chef, I took the liberty of making a special dessert today. One I thought we might share."

"That sounds great," I replied.

She smiled. "It isn't often we have visitors as nice as you. This town is historical and old. Unfortunately, so are almost all the residents."

We walked together through the snow.

"Grant, I'm in my late twenties. I get very bored and lonely being snowed in, waiting until spring arrives."

I nodded my head. I was lonely too.

"Let's go back to my cottage and I'll boil some water, make some tea. This will taste good with the blueberry-peach cobbler and fresh whipped cream I prepared for us."

"Your offer is too good to resist. I'll lead the way," I replied. My mouth was watering.

As we approached the cottage, I spotted a group of deer eating berries by the front door. The roof of the cottage had lots of snow from the night before. There was a large pine tree near the driveway with soft drifts of snow on all the branches. Smoke came from the chimney, and it smelled really wonderful.

When I commented on that, Ursula said, "I use several different types of wood to give it a smell that I find relaxing."

"I think the deer like it too."

She laughed.

As I walked into the sweet-smelling cottage, Ursula said, "Make yourself comfortable in front of the fireplace. I'm taking the cobbler out of the oven, and I'm going to boil some water for our tea."

I took off my boots and hung my coat on the rack by the door. Then I walked over to the couch and sat down. I thought, "I must be dreaming. Maybe I'm still asleep in Dr. Siegfried's guest room."

Ursula called me into the kitchen. "I want to get out of these damp clothes. I was chopping wood, and I'm soaked all the way through. Just watch the stove for me, make sure the water doesn't boil over."

"Of course," I said.

As the water started to boil, so did my blood, my pulse racing. I was picturing how Ursula would look in something much more comfortable.

A few minutes later, she came back in the kitchen in a short pink nightgown. Her hair was down, and she looked at me and smiled.

She turned off the stove, and made our tea. Then she grinned at me and said, "Are you ready for dessert?"

I smiled and said yes as I reached for her. I grabbed her around the waist and pulled her to me, then I kissed her. I slid off her gown and began to devour her, kissing, smelling, tasting, and licking every part of her body like a hungry wolf tenderizing dinner right before an eating frenzy. Just looking at her fed my soul.

We went to her bedroom and lay down. Ursula became more and more submissive to my touch. I grabbed her hair like a horse's rein. The mirror across from the bed allowed me to watch us as the night progressed. I could see evolution happening.

After a couple of hours, Ursula and I lay together in total bliss. Gradually our breathing became shallow and easy as we began to breathe in sync. We were wrapped in a thick, oversized comforter, and it was as if we were in a cocoon, embraced in each other's arms. Our body heat acted like a furnace, keeping us warm. We were safe from the outside world.

It felt as if we had melted together and become one. One with nature, and one with the peaceful universe around us.

In the morning, Ursula made Belgian waffles with fresh maple syrup. She brewed a pot of hazelnut coffee. We spoke of the genuine connection between us, and agreed that it was undeniable.

But I had to go for therapy and Ursula needed to go to work. We walked back to the main house together, holding hands. It was a beautiful morning. The air was crisp, clean, and easy to breathe.

As we walked over the footbridge, Dr. Siegfried stood watching us through the lab window. I said, "I'll see you later."

Ursula smiled and walked toward the kitchen.

When I entered the laboratory, Dr. Siegfried said, "I trust you were in good hands for the evening?"

"Yes, very good hands." I replied.

Dr. Siegfried said, "Excellent. Now it is time for more treatments."

As the days went on, I became more energetic, more vibrant, and much more healthy. Soon I felt well enough to head home.

I decided to visit my mother in Florida. I planned to stay for only a short while, before heading on to New York.

CHAPTER 12

FLORIDA

When I landed in Miami, the sun was shining, the air was warm, and the ocean looked gorgeous. The sun felt good on my skin, especially with temperatures of eighty degrees rather than twenty.

I had the car service drop me off in South Beach, where my friend Len met me for lunch. He was living near Lincoln Road. He said, "Stay at my place, I have an extra guest room."

I agreed to stay for a while. I needed to recover from my jetlag, and I was up for some beachfront R&R.

We got in Len's little sports car and he drove to his place. To my surprise, he pulled up to an enormous mansion. "This is my place. It used to be the home of a big deal mobster. I'm renting it, I'm friends with the new owner."

"This is great!" I was impressed. The house was beautiful, an Art Deco gem.

The interior décor combined Deco with Art Nouveau. Teal, turquoise, sea foam, beige, and pink were the main colors and all the rooms were high ceilinged and bright. Palm trees of many types were scattered around the massive property.

"I have some friends coming over in a little while," Len said.

"Okay, great. So which way to the guest room?"

Len said, "I'll show you."

He led me to a palatial bedroom with a canopy bed and mirrors on the walls. I said, "This is awesome!"

He said to meet him downstairs when I was ready. I put my bags away and got settled in, which took me about five minutes. Then I went downstairs.

I couldn't find Len. The house was immense, one room leading to another leading to another. I called out, "Len where are you?"

I heard him laugh. He said, "Follow my voice; I'm in the living room."

I walked into a ballroom with a pool table in the center. Len said, "Are you any good at pool?"

"I'm okay." It had been a while since I'd played, but I did like the game.

He racked up the balls, and we shot pool until the doorbell rang.

Len said, "Can you get the door?"

"If I can find it," I replied.

When I opened the door, four of the most beautiful women I had ever seen were waiting on the other side. Blondes with tans were smiling at me.

Len came up behind me. "Ladies! Welcome. Come in, come in. I want you to meet my friend Grant. We need to show Grant how to relax Miami style."

So they did.

The next morning Len's girlfriend made breakfast.

It was a beautiful day, so Len and I decided to take a ride down Ocean Drive.

As we cruised along, Len said, "Tell me about your adventures in Bavaria. How was it living in an old castle? I have a million questions!"

I told him, "Look, it's a long story."

He laughed. "We have the time. I'm not doing anything today, and I'm all ears!"

I looked at him and laughed. I said, "Let's get some coffee first."

"Then you'll tell me everything?"

"I'll tell you *some* things."

"No, I want to know everything that happened."

I shrugged. "I'll try, but my memory is getting foggier as we speak. Besides, I think it's almost lunchtime."

"Grant, you just ate breakfast. Remember the nice omelet Linda cooked for us?"

"It was cute, just like your girlfriend, but now it's time to *really* eat. Take me somewhere we can chow down."

"Okay, okay. I know just the place," he said.

We went to an authentic diner where the breakfast specials were served all day long. After we ordered, Len said, "Okay, food's on the way, so you can at least start your story."

I laughed. He was persistent. "All right, so I purchased a ticket to Bavaria—"

"Hey Len!"

We turned around and there was this gorgeous, sexy woman. She smiled at Len and he jumped up. He went over, hugged and kissed her, and invited her to join us for breakfast.

He said to me, "Grant, this is Jessica."

She smiled at me. "Nice to meet you."

"Likewise," I replied.

"Grant just came back from Bavaria and he was about to tell me all about his trip."

I replied, "Yes, I was, but here comes breakfast."

Len looked at me and laughed. "You know you're going to tell me your story before this day is over, right?"

I said, "I know," and smiled devilishly, which made Jessica laugh.

Len said, "Jessica, I've been trying to get Grant to tell me about his trip all morning, but he won't!"

"Why not?" Jessica asked.

"Because Grant needed coffee, then he needed something to eat. For the second time this morning!"

We all laughed.

I said, "Jessica, it's true. I'm still adjusting to the time differences."

She smiled. "Len, I like your friend."

This made me laugh even more, because Len really wanted to strangle me for that.

I said, "After breakfast, let's walk down Lincoln Road and I'll tell you about my adventures in Bavaria."

Len said, "If I get the check, do you promise to tell us everything?"

I smiled, and said, "Yes, everything!"

But when I giggled, Len said, "What was that for?"

I said, "Oh, nothing," and Jessica started to laugh.

After we finished eating, Len paid the bill and we walked over to Lincoln Road. I told them about the German doctor, his special therapies, the beautiful estate, and my improved health.

Len and Jessica seemed mesmerized by my story. They looked at each other and then back at me. Len said, "Oh my god, bro, that's fucking amazing!"

Jessica said, "I didn't know these types of therapies even existed."

I nodded. "I didn't either until I went over there and got treated. Now I feel *so* good. In fact, I've never felt better in my life."

As I said this, I realized it was true. My energy was incredible, my appetite enormous, my zest for life increased exponentially. It was a miracle.

"I want to feel good too! " Len said.

"But you look fine," I replied.

"No, bro, I'm tired all the time. I know I could feel better than this," he complained.

"Let's talk more about this later," I replied.

Jessica said, "Look, in the tree. A flock of green parrots."

I looked up and saw them gathered in a coconut palm tree. They were making a lot of noise. They took off, yakking. They traveled about in groups, flying from tree to tree and squawking.

We walked into some really cool little shops where they sold sunglasses, jewelry, designer clothing, and artwork. The people walking around were runway model beautiful. Each one who passed us was more beautiful than the last. So many were tall and tanned, they all looked like Hollywood stars.

Jessica had to go meet up with some clients. She said she would drop by the house later.

Len and I walked around some more.

I said, "Len, do you know about the Bermuda triangle?"

"Yes, of course, it's out in the ocean not far from here."

"You're almost right."

"*Almost* right?" He gave me a questioning look.

"The Bermuda triangle reaches from Haulover Beach all the way to 13th Street, then west all the way to Biscayne Bay."

"Impossible," he said. He pulled out his phone and looked it up. Then he looked at me with wide eyes. "Oh my god! Grant, you're right! I can't believe this!"

I nodded. "They say if you're there at the right time, very strange things may happen. Because you are inside some sort of magnetic anomaly."

He made a face. "Bro, how do you know all this?"

I smiled and winked. "I'll tell you more tonight, if you round up some more women!"

"No problem."

We went back to the house where Len made some phone calls. I decided to take a shower, lie down for a while, recharge. A short while later, I heard him yelling, "Grant, Grant, time to wake up!"

"I'm awake, but I don't see you. Where are you?"

He laughed. "I'm on the intercom near your door. Come down to the kitchen."

As I headed downstairs, the aroma of hazelnut coffee wafted my way. I ran down the stairs and into the kitchen. Len stood by the counter brewing coffee. "It smells amazing throughout the whole house. I need a cup of that right now!"

"I made it for you," Len said. "I made us a full pot because we have a chance to talk before, um; we get together with our *company*."

He grinned and poured me a cup. Then we sat down on the patio lounge which had giant cushions, umbrellas on tables, and piped-in reggae music. The sun felt great, warm but not searing.

Len asked, "So how did you know to go to Europe and get those special treatments?"

I sipped my coffee. "That's another long story."

We sat in the sun and drank our coffee as I told my friend in greater detail about the trip and what I'd experienced.

"Oh my god, this is too much for my mind to comprehend," Len said. "I have to think about it."

His phone rang so he took the call. A minute later, he told me, "Hey, we're invited to go meet the ladies at this cool club on Collins. After we have a few drinks, we're all coming back here for more fun." Sounded good to me! "

CHAPTER 13

THE NEW BUSINESS

At the club on Collins, I was introduced to a beautiful woman. Mielle was a botanist and she traveled around the world collecting flowers, shrubs, plants, and tree samples. She used the samples to make her own all-natural fragrances, as well as other organic products for the face and body.

I was impressed. I asked her if she had any samples of her products.

"Yes," she replied. "Here, smell this." And she brought a vial up to my nose.

The fragrance was deeply beautiful, enrapturing. It smelled like it was freshly pressed, the essence of an exotic flower captured and retained perfectly. When I closed my eyes I had visions of an exotic location near the ocean, on a mountain top where the flowers grew wild. The colors of these particular flowers were bright and happy as they thrived in a tranquil environment.

As I held the vial in my hand and smelled the essence, the images in my mind became clearer. I gradually became intoxicated by the flower essence. My breathing was more relaxed and rhythmic, linked now to my emotions. It was as if my emotions and my body gently and easily synchronized, aligned as one in harmony. Like I was wrapped in a blanket of bliss.

As I opened my eyes, I saw the palm trees swaying and I heard the fronds brushing together. I had a whole new perspective on life in which my heart and mind felt open. I was ready for a new adventure, whether it was meeting new people or traveling to a mountain top, somewhere I had never been before.

Instantly, I knew I *had* to do something with these amazing products.

"Mielle, would you consider allowing me to become a distributor for your products?" I asked.

She stared at me, her large eyes unblinking. "I'm very selective about things like this," she replied.

"I understand," I said. Who wouldn't be with a product line so incredible? We exchanged numbers.

A few weeks went by before she called me. "I liked meeting you, Grant, " Mielle said. "I decided I do want you as my distributor."

"Great!" I was excited.

I launched my business right away. I formed a small company, built a website, and created a beautiful catalog. I started meeting a lot of people, exchanging business cards and telling them about the products. Unfortunately, the marketplace was saturated, controlled by the big corporations with lots of money. So I went to Palm Beach to speak to some friends I thought might be able to help.

I borrowed Len's car and drove up the coast. The ocean was calm, a beautiful shade of blue-green where the sun reflected off the water. Brown pelicans were diving for fish, and the road was free of traffic.

I met my friend Pier and his wife Julie at a well-known establishment in town. I told them about the product line and showed them some samples. They loved the products, but Pier said the economy was fragile so investors wanted to hold on to whatever they had. "You may have to wait a few years, until things get better with the economy," he warned.

On my way back from Palm Beach, I stopped at my mother's. She looked great. We went out for dinner and I had told her what was happening with my life in Miami.

ABOUT MY MOM

Lillian was born in the Bronx in 1936 and grew up on Morris Avenue. When she was three, her father divorced my grandmother. So Lillian had no real recollection of her father. His name was Morris, just like the street they lived on.

My grandmother worked late shifts as a nurse and a waitress. So she wasn't home much, and my mother was left alone most of the time. My mother spent most of her time down the block with her friend Francine. At Francine's house, the family watched over my mother and treated her like another daughter.

In her early twenties, Lillian landed a job at a famous cosmetic, a very successful cosmetics company on Fifth Avenue. She was an executive there for many years.

When the neighborhood in the Bronx became too dangerous, my mother left. She rented an apartment on Ocean Parkway in Brooklyn for only a little more than what my grandmother was paying. My grandmother finally came to her senses and moved to Brooklyn to a nice neighborhood, where she lived for the next forty-three years.

While working for this tremendous corporation, Lillian went to many parties and events. At one of these parties, she met my dad. She liked him, but not enough to give him the right telephone number!

At the time she was dating another man. David was wealthy; he came from a well-to-do family. He wanted to marry Lillian. But Lillian thought David wanted to the mold her to fit into his family and his circle of friends. She didn't want to be anything other than herself.

One night she went with Francine to a dance. My dad was there. He spotted Lillian and took her hand, guiding her onto the dance floor. My dad was the only man she could be herself with, she told me later, and he made her laugh.

As they were dancing, he said, "That was cute, Lillian. You gave me the wrong phone number!"

Lillian laughed. She liked him. She said, "Bill, here's my real number."

He was a ballroom dance instructor, so he taught her how to dance. They won many awards together in competitions. Through her job, Lillian was able to get tickets and the best seats to all the Broadway shows. The two of them loved to go to Broadway; they loved watching all those shows.

They eventually married. She left her job and they moved to Long Island.

I stayed at my mother's condo that night. We planned to eat breakfast together before I headed back to South Beach.

But we never made it to breakfast. In the morning she told me she wasn't feeling well, so I took her to see her doctor. Her blood pressure was high so he ordered an electrocardiogram.

The EKG results were abnormal, so the doctor called an ambulance to take my mother to the hospital. I immediately called my brother. "Mom is being rushed to the hospital in town. I need you here."

Stephen said, "I'm getting in my car right now. I'll be there as soon as possible."

The cardiologist said he needed to do further testing. My brother arrived, so we went out for breakfast. We were very upset, nervous and worried.

When my brother and I returned to the hospital, our mother had been transferred to an emergency cardiac unit. It took the hospital two weeks to figure out what was wrong with her.

We waited and waited while she grew weaker and weaker. She looked at me one day and said, "Grant, you're right!

"About what?"

"I should've listened to you and purchased a mediocre insurance policy, but instead I bought the best. Now they're milking it while torturing me nonstop with their needles and tests, never letting me rest. If I would've listened to you and purchased a cheaper policy, I would've been released by now. I'd be relaxing at home, watching TV."

I replied, "Probably, but we have to deal with the present, not the 'I could have' or 'I should have.'"

"I know I'm supposed to eat, but the IV medication is making me so nauseous. I have to force myself to take a bite of something."

Each meal looked and smelled worse than the one before. So I started bringing her fresh food from local restaurants. But as the days dragged on, she grew weaker from the lousy food, the lack of rest, the stressful waiting.

Then the inevitable happened. She developed a blood clot in her arm.

The open heart surgery was postponed until the clot dissolved. Blood thinners were administered intravenously, along with several other medications.

After nine days, the blood clot had dissolved by eighty percent. The doctors claimed that this type of clot was not as dangerous because it was near the surface of the skin, so it was less likely to travel through the body to pose a threat. They were ready to repair her heart valves and address critical vessels.

I questioned the doctors in charge. "I don't think my mom is strong enough to undergo this type of surgery."

The primary care physician said, "If your mother doesn't have this surgery, her days will be numbered."

The usual medical scare tactics.

I replied, "But if she does, her days might numbered even less! Why would you even consider operating on a woman in this type of weakened condition?"

The doctor replied, "Because she needs the surgery."

I said, "Okay, so I want to put *you* on the same IV drip that kills your appetite, and I want to wake you up every two hours to draw blood for tests. At the same time, you will not be allowed to leave your bed. We'll do this to you for two weeks and then, while your body is in starvation mode and in a state of utter exhaustion, I'll have the cardiac surgeon instruct the anesthesiologist to put you under so he can take a bone saw to your sternum and crack you open like a broiled lobster. All this whether you need the surgery or not. Are you okay with this, Doctor?"

The doctor looked stunned. He turned and hurried off. I yelled after him, "Think *you* would live? What makes you think a seventy-eight year old woman will?"

The hospital staff in the hallway turned around to stare at me. I saw a look in their eyes, a kind of acknowledgment, an understanding that I'd hit a bull's-eye. I could see the tears in some of the nurses' eyes. The surgeon looked ashamed, sad for me. He was the only doctor there who actually listened to me, someone I considered human. Not like the other money-hungry doctors. The two cardiologists working with my mother had a superiority complex, and they both behaved as if they were gods.

My mother signed off on the surgery. The following Monday, my brother and I paced around in the waiting room for eight and half hours.

The surgeon came down to speak with us afterward. "The surgery was a success. Your mother's heart looks great. But it will take a couple of months for her to recover. She will need rehabilitation."

We were relieved.

When we arrived at her room she was still unconscious, doped up, intubated on a ventilator. The gash in her chest was like something out of a science fiction movie, along with all the machines and equipment they'd hooked up.

As the days went on, her condition progressively worsened. She was not able to breathe on her own and could not be weaned off the ventilator. It was as though I was living through my grandmother's horrific suffering all over again.

My mother was turning yellow due to jaundice from liver failure. The doctors claimed she'd had liver failure before she entered the hospital. What a farce! Soon enough, her kidneys stopped working, the bladder collapsed, her lungs began to fill with fluid, and her brain seized.

Later, I did some investigational work on the drugs that were administered. One particular drug may cause heart failure, liver failure, kidney failure, as well as lung and brain damage. It virtually destroys the organs of those it is administered to. The side effects are all well-known, yet the mechanism of how it works to support the cardiac rhythm is unknown. This drug peaks at three weeks and cannot be excreted by the liver or the kidneys; those who receive it must wait fifty-six days for a turnover of new cells in order to survive, provided this poisonous drug has been discontinued before the patient's organs shut down.

Who Okayed This?!

The corruption of medical politics sickened me. I found it disgusting and inhumane. Still, the doctors got their money, as did the hospitals, pharmacies, and drug corporations.

After consulting with four prominent attorneys, I discovered that legislation had been passed so that, if a patient over the age of sixty-five was in critical condition and there was no spouse and children were over the age of twenty-five, the surviving children had no grounds for a lawsuit to defend the living or deceased. This gave hospitals and their doctors a veil of protection. They could go ahead and do what they wanted to our loved ones.

Who Okayed This?!

In my grief, I wondered if the surgery was botched and that's why they chose to administer the toxic drug. The only other conclusion would be that, with the myriad of pharmaceuticals, they needed guinea pigs to test them on. Sounded like sci-fi but that's medical politics.

My friend's mother died in the exact same fashion as my beloved dog Scotty. They were both administered a diuretic, and then injected with the same toxic steroidal anti-inflammatory. These two drugs should never be mixed together. In both instances, the combination caused cardiac failure. This happened to both loved ones in the same year.

Who Okayed This?!

I asked the entire staff of doctors tending my mother, ranging from the cardiologist to the primary care physician and the cardiac thoracic surgeon, a question that none of them could answer. The question was: What are you doing to address the mitochondria?

The medical staff appeared dumbfounded, scratching their heads. Only a physician's assistant responded. She said, "Nothing. We don't know how to do that here."

I told them the mitochondria are within every cell, all the cells that make up every organ in the body, which in turn keep us functioning and alive. The mitochondria were the batteries of the body. I said to all of these health professionals, "Don't you think addressing the mitochondria is important?"

They avoided me.

It had dawned on me after my mother's untimely death that this toxin had taken residency within all of Lillian's mitochondria, causing cellular paralysis, thereby causing her cellular metabolism to produce apoptosis. She had perished from the very core of her very being.

What the scientific researchers should have been working on is something to shrink the swollen egos of the medical establishment and those other greedy and uncaring forces destroying everything on this planet.

My heart was broken. I stayed in my mother's condo taking care of her business and grieving yet another loss.

CHAPTER 14

STEVE

A guy named Steve moved in next door. In his sixties, Steve came down from New Jersey. He called it "Jersey." A nice guy, he smiled all the time and laughed a lot.

He spoke to me every day about my product line. He was interested in helping me with my business venture. He wanted to get involved in building up my clientele. We drank coffee, brainstormed ideas, talked about how to best market the natural essences.

The skin care business I had launched was small, but it had a lot of potential. I had organic products that were different than most of the stuff on the market. I wanted to add a line of organic cosmetics.

Steve and I were able to locate a compound formulator who worked for a large manufacturer. They had everything I needed, so the new cosmetic line could easily be developed. I just had to figure out a marketing plan and a way to capitalize the venture.

I had a friend who sold magnets. Mr. Magnets told me he knew a beautiful model in Miami named Tamara. I explained to him that I needed models for publicity purposes in order to launch the line of products.

Mr. Magnets set up a meeting so that I could meet with her. Steve came with me.

We met Tamara in South Beach in a posh lounge at a hip hotel the celebrities frequented. She was six feet tall, well built, and gorgeous. She'd been a model for many years. Her perfect features were simply stunning.

As I ordered coffee, Tamara received a phone call that made her smile from ear to ear.

She hung up and said, "I'm going to be in a new movie! I get to play the role of the main character's hair stylist. It's a huge production! And it's going to film right here, in Miami."

"Wow! Congratulations!" I said.

Her smile was dazzling. "Mr. Magnets told me a little about what you're doing, Grant. How can I be of assistance?"

"We need exposure, so we plan to do some promotional work which involves models."

Tamara said, "I'll call some of my contacts and my model friends and see what I can stir up." She told us she had other appointments and had to go. "I'll keep you posted, and call you during the week," she promised.

A week later, Tamara called. "Grant, its fashion week in Miami. I have a pass for you and Steve at the door at the W so you can get in to see the fashion show. I want to introduce you to some important people who may be able to help you."

I was excited. The W was a super fancy hotel. They had chic parties. A fashion show there sounded like a good entree.

She told me to meet her in the club for the show. "After the runway show, there's a party across the street. I'll introduce you to some of the right people."

On Saturday I was having my first cup of coffee when Steve called. He asked, "Are you ready?"

I said, "Steve, it's nine thirty in the morning! We don't have to be in Miami until this evening."

He started laughing. "I know, I know, I'm just excited about everything. But maybe we should leave early and get a head start?"

"Steve, relax, it's not even ten yet. And we're not in a race."

He laughed. "I am! I'm in a race to see Tamara again! I couldn't stop thinking about her all week."

I sighed. "She's married, and besides, this is business."

Steve said, "I know, I know. But she'll be there tonight, right?"

"Yes, Steve, and she's going to introduce us to a lot of important people."

"Okay, okay, I'll call you in a few hours. We better leave early to beat all the weekend traffic."

I said okay but I was laughing. He was *so* ready to go.

Steve said, "I have nothing to eat in the house. Maybe we could leave soon and stop somewhere, get something to eat before we arrive at the show?"

"Okay, we could do that," I replied, still chuckling.

A few hours later, I was showered and ready to go. Apparently Steve was too because he was sitting in front of my house in his car. I grabbed some product samples, put them in gift bags, checked my hair, and hurried out the door.

It was in the mid-nineties, and with the humidity it felt like a hundred and four. When I slid into the passenger seat of Steve's car, the air conditioner was blasting.

He smiled, shook my hand. "Cold enough in here for you?"

I replied, "Steve, maybe we should turn it up a notch?" It felt like fifty-five degrees in his car. I could see the cold air coming out of the vents as if someone had opened a freezer door.

Steve laughed at the expression on my face, and said, "So ok, I'll turn it down. I'm anxious to get to Miami on time to see my girl!"

I laughed. "What girl, Steve?"

He pulled away from the curb and drove down the street. "You know, my girl Tamara."

I looked at his happy face and laughed. "Steve, she is not your girl, and this is supposed to be business."

"I know, I know. But I'm going to make her my girl."

I shook my head. "Steve, you're crazy, man."

"Oh yeah. I'm crazy all right. Crazy in love!"

"In love? But you just met her."

"That's all it takes sometimes. Haven't you ever been in love?" he asked.

"Yes, of course. But with someone I knew!"

We both laughed. "You better conduct yourself professionally," I said.

"I will, I will, don't worry about me. I'll be fine. As long as my girl's there."

"Maybe I should go alone?"

He laughed. "I'm just having fun with you. I gassed up the car, the AC is blasting, and there's tickets waiting at the door. With our names on them!" He paused, said, "I *am* invited, right?"

"Right."

Steve said, "Let's stop for soup and a burger."

"That sounds good; I haven't eaten a thing since five-thirty this morning."

"I had some instant oatmeal, if you want to call that a meal," Steve said as he pulled into an empty parking space.

We walked into the neighborhood deli and had a nice lunch. After we ate, Steve looked at me and said, "I'm so full, all I want do is lay down and go to sleep for a few hours. We better stop and get some coffee to go."

I replied, "Roger that. You don't have to ask *me* twice."

Right down the street was a drive-through so we ordered up two coffees.

Steve handed me a cardboard cup. "Be careful, it's boiling hot!" He put his coffee between us in the cup holder.

I said, "Steve, why don't you try your coffee before we go?"

He shook his head. "I can't. I'm sure it's too hot, like yours."

We were halfway down the road and stopped at a red light when he decided to see if he could drink his coffee. He popped off the lid and took a big slurp. "Christmas! This coffee's terrible, and it's ice cold."

I couldn't control my laughter when I saw his sour expression.

We turned around and went back to the coffee shop. When we pulled up to the drive-through window, Steve said to the server, "I just bought this coffee and it's terrible. How can you serve black coffee ice cold?"

People inside the coffee shop were laughing.

The server handed Steve a new cup of coffee. She said, "Here, try this." He took a sip and said, "Oh, now *that's* hot coffee!" He thanked her and peeled out, his tires screeching.

I was laughing. The guy was sixty-two!

We pulled onto I-95 and headed for South Beach. It was a beautiful evening. The sky was clear, the moon bright, the night air sultry. As he was driving, Steve smiled in anticipation like a kid in a candy shop.

When we arrived in South Beach, the streets were lit up with neon, the buildings modeled in the stylish Art Deco fashion. It was hopping, crowds milling everywhere.

Steve said, "Wow! Look at this place, it's amazing! Are we nearby, are we close to the hotel where the party is? Because I don't want to miss seeing my girl!"

I felt like slapping him. He knew this, and it made him laugh.

I directed him to the hotel entrance. As we pulled up to the front in order to valet park, the view was lovely. The front of the hotel was pink and blue, complemented by swaying green palm trees. The starry night added glints of light.

"It's a gorgeous night. Who could ask for anything more?" I said.

Steve replied, "I can. My girl! Let's go in the hotel so I can find her."

I rolled my eyes. We walked inside the hotel lobby and over to the club entrance. Steve attempted to walk past security without checking in.

When security stopped him, I said "Steve, you're crazy! Relax, we'll get in, we're on the list."

The security guy looked for our names on the list. They weren't there.

Steve looked at me with desperation on his face. "Now what? I hope we didn't drive all the way here for nothing."

I pulled him aside, told him to relax. I texted Tamara. She texted me back: "No worries, be right there."

Tamara greeted us with a big smile and told security we were her guests. The guard shrugged and said okay, so we headed inside.

The theme was neon. There were models everywhere wearing neon outfits, neon makeup, neon shoes and accessories. The models were tall and thin, very beautiful.

I said to Steve, "What do you think?"

He said, "I think I'm going to have a heart attack right here. That is, unless I've died already and gone to heaven."

I laughed.

He said, "These girls are so beautiful, if I dropped dead right here, I'd be satisfied just because I had the chance to stand next to some of them."

Tamara giggled. Then she said, "Guys, I have to get up on the runway now. I'll catch up with you two later."

Steve said goodbye. He looked around the room, taking it all in. His tongue was hanging out of his mouth.

I said "Steve, Steve... Steve!"

He had gone into a trance. When he finally responded, he said, "Grant, I'm sorry, I'm speechless and in love."

"In love with Tamara?"

"I don't know who I'm in love with anymore, they're all so beautiful."

"Steve, you look like you're someplace far away with that goofy smile of yours," I said.

"I am far away, I'm in heaven!"

I was starting to worry. How could he conduct business in this sex trance of his? I said, "Steve, we have to do business, so get your act together!"

He laughed. "I'll try but it will be hard with so many gorgeous girls, one after the other, saying hello to me. And dressed in those outfits? I better get a few beer muscles in me to calm me down."

"Do whatever it takes, but don't get drunk, this is business," I said.

"Okay, okay, don't worry about me. I've been around a while; I can handle a few cold ones."

I went to the restroom. Then I went outside to make a few phone calls. When I walked back into the club, Steve was doing shots of double malt Scotch.

I ran over to the bar. "Steve, slow down! We still have to go to the party afterwards to talk with people and do business."

"Okay, okay," Steve replied drunkenly.

Tamara came up to me. "We're all going to meet across the street to the other club.

We're having the after show party there."

"That sounds good," I said. "How's the food?"

She replied, "Amazing! I'm hungry after preparing for this show. I'm not just modeling tonight, you know. I'm helping manage the show, making sure everything is running smoothly."

"You're doing a great job," I told her. "The show is magnificent."

She hugged me and gave me a kiss.

Steve saw this and moved toward us, but he fell over a bar stool in the process. He landed on the floor, right at Tamara's feet. He straightened his glasses, laughing as he stood up.

Tamara asked, "Steve, are you alright?"

"Yes! I guess I fell over something?"

Tamara said, "You fell over a barstool, Steven."

He replied, "That's not all I'm falling for. You're so beautiful; it's worth getting a few bruises to see you up close."

She blushed and laughed. A few other models overheard and giggled as they walked by. Tamara said, "Thank you, Steven, but I need you in one piece for the party across the street."

"You can count on me," Steve replied. "I'm going to splash my face with some cold water, spruce up," he told me. Then he headed for the men's room.

Tamara said to me, "Where did you *find* him?"

I replied, "He's my neighbor."

We both laughed. Then she said, "I like him. He's funny."

After he cleaned up in the restroom, Steve headed for the hotel coffee shop. He ordered a large hot coffee, and sat down in a booth. That's where I joined him.

He said, "Those women must think I'm crazy."

I said, "They don't just think so, they *know* you're crazy."

After we stopped laughing, I said, "The party starts in twenty minutes. Think you'll be ready to talk with people and do some business?"

"Yeah, of course. I know what I'm doing. After all, I've been on this earth longer than you have."

"That's for sure."

"So don't underestimate an old bastard like me. You'd be surprised, Grant. Some of these executives are my age so I can relate better because I'm from their generation."

I nodded. "You're probably right."

Steve said with a little smile, "I like to think that I know what I'm talking about, at least some of the time."

I said, "You should, you've been walking this planet a long time."

Then I told him my dad used to say that to me all the time. He said, "Yours and mine both."

When he finished the coffee, he stood up and said, "Okay, okay, let's get going. We have models to meet!"

"Remember we're here for business first and foremost. Tamara is trying to help us, and we are at this party tonight because of her. But she didn't invite us to go after models, she got us in here to meet people of means," I said.

"I know, you're right," Steve said. "So let's go to the party."

I wasn't sure if he got it or not. I rolled my eyes and followed him out of the coffee shop.

Steve said, "Wow! It's perfect out tonight." All the restaurants, clubs, and hotels were blazing with light and the street was filled with people in short shorts and short skirts.

We made our way to the restaurant. This time security didn't pose a problem. We were on the guest list for the party, so we strolled right in.

The runway models clustered in small groups, along with Hollywood stars and local actress/model types. We were gawking, both of us.

Tamara called out, "Grant, Steve, over here!"

We headed over to her table. Tamara said, "Mary, this is Grant and Steven."

Mary said, "I take it you enjoy watching models on the runway?"

Steve replied, "Am I awake? These girls are so gorgeous; I thought I must be dreaming. Maybe I've left the planet!"

Mary laughed and said, "What planet do you think you're on?"

"The women here are so beautiful, I don't care. Whichever planet I'm on, I want to stick around for a while."

Mary said, "Have you met any of the girls?"

"Well, I met Tamara, and that's a big deal for me."

Mary and Tamara laughed. Then they said they would show us around and introduce both of us to some of the women.

It was one beautiful woman after another. Finally, Steve looked at me and said, "I can't take it anymore!"

I laughed. "What do you mean? These women are what dreams are made of. "

He shrugged and said, "Grant, you have to understand. I'm from Jersey. I never got this close to such beautiful women before. This is like something you see in the movies!"

Tamara came over with a woman named Wendy. We introduced ourselves. Wendy told us she had her own radio show where she could help us advertise and get our product name out there. We chatted with her for a while, and then exchanged business cards.

Tamara then introduced us to Eileen. She was very beautiful, and knowledgeable about the beauty industry. We gave her some samples of our products as well as our business cards.

We finally met Tamara's heavy hitter. Lawrence invested in small business ventures and large hedge funds. He had done well for himself. A handsome man around Steve's age, Lawrence got right to the point. He asked Steve, "How are your numbers this quarter? What does your portfolio look like?"

Steve said, "We have a great business plan but, to tell you the truth, we're just starting out with our product line."

Lawrence frowned. "That could be a bit if a problem if you're looking for capital. Any investor is going to want to see some numbers, at least the annual and quarterly figures."

Steve looked at me, then said, "Well, we're a startup business looking for somebody who will give us a chance. Just think, you can get in on the ground floor!"

He shook his head. "With the way the economy is, not many people want to gamble with their investments. Not without seeing profit and loss statements." He shrugged. "I'm sorry, but I'm out for now. Here's my card. Call me when you get more established."

We kept trying to interest people, but we hit this same brick wall over and over that evening. In Miami, there was a lot of competition and not much venture capital.

We had a great night anyway.

At one point I went to the men's room. Steve decided to have a drink at the bar. When I came out, I walked into the bar. An older, sophisticated looking woman was chatting with Steve. They exchanged numbers, and then she walked away.

Steve made his way over to where I was standing by the tiki bar. He said, "Did you see that?"

"Yes, and it looked like you were having a fine time."

He said, "She was nice, but with all these young women here, I don't have time for that."

I said, "Steve, it doesn't look like these younger women are knocking down your door, does it?" Then I laughed.

"Laugh it up, Grant."

Tamara walked over. "Steve, do you have any idea who you were just talking to?"

Steve nodded. "Her name is Ruthie. We kidded around, and then we exchanged numbers."

Tamara lifted a brow. "You exchanged numbers?"

"Yeah. What's the big deal isn't that what people do?"

"Yes, but Steve, here's the thing. You know her name is Ruthie, but what you don't know is she owns several oil refineries. And this building!"

Steve spit out a mouthful of beer. It flew everywhere, splashing down the front of his shirt. He straightened his glasses and said, "Are you shitting me?"

Tamara smirked. "You didn't even look at her business card, did you?"

"No, and I was going to throw her card in the glove compartment or on the floor of my car with all the other forgotten business cards."

Tamara and I laughed. She said, "Ruthie hardly ever talks with people she doesn't know. She must really like you if she gave you her number. So you better call her."

He nodded his face serious.

I said, "See, Steve, you did better than you thought tonight."

Steve laughed. "I'm guarding this card with my life!" He took it out of his back pocket and tucked it into a sleeve in his wallet.

At the end of the evening, Tamara walked us outside. "I hope you guys had fun tonight. And I hope some of the people I introduced you to will work out for the company. I'll call you sometime next week. Drive safe."

I thanked her and Steve said, "I can't get this dumb grin off my face. Thank you, Tamara, for the best night of my life!"

She smiled and waved good bye.

The valet brought our car around and handed Steve the keys. He passed them to me. "You're driving because I sure as shit can't get behind the wheel."

I drove down Collins, and we stopped off to get a bite to eat before venturing home. At a quiet diner, we both ordered eggs and coffee. Steve was still smiling from ear to ear.

I said, "Well, I guess you had a nice time tonight."

He nodded. "I found my future wife."

"Don't get ahead of yourself," I replied.

He sipped his coffee. "Grant, what did you think of Ruthie?"

"I didn't speak to her, but I thought she was pretty. Come to think of it, she did have some nice legs on her too."

Steve replied, "Hey, careful, that's my girl you're talking about. I'm in love, man, so watch what you say."

"Steve, you fall in love at the drop of a hat."

"I know, I know. But this time, can you blame me? Think about where we just came from, where we were all night. The hotel, the restaurant, the people, the glitz. The lifestyle!"

He was right. Ruthie was some catch.

We finished our breakfast and drove home as the sun rose in the perfect blue sky.

Steve called Ruthie the next day. They made a date for the following evening. They fell in love and became a committed couple.

So Steve started a new life with Ruthie and, even though we remained friends, he dropped out of the business.

I continued on, growing the business by myself.

CHAPTER 15

SOCIAL MEDIA

Life in Florida suited me. In fact, life was good. Then an old acquaintance found me on Facebook. I had gone to school with Sam nearly thirty years before. We were never friends, but we knew one another.

Sam emailed me and said he lived nearby. He wanted to meet for coffee and reminisce about Long Island and mutual friends. I figured it would be harmless to meet him and chat for an hour or so.

Upon arriving at the café where we'd agreed to meet, I looked around. It took me a while to find him. I didn't recognize him. He looked prematurely old, his sparse hair gray, his bald pate showing through. He had a horrible, haunted look about him, as if he carried the world on his back.

We spoke about the old days. Sam was familiar with my business and had checked out my website. He asked a lot of questions about the products.

After our brief meeting, he called constantly. I was curt; I could tell he was interested in the business, not me. He finally gave it a rest and stopped calling.

A week later, Sam called. "Hey, I'm going to my friend's club tonight. You want to meet up for a drink?"

I didn't, but I had been looking for something to do. So why not?

I told him, "I don't drink alcohol, but I'll come check out your friend's club."

When I arrived, the club was crowded. The owners seemed nice. Sam said, "I want to introduce you to someone else, Grant. My friend Alan. I think he can help you with your business."

When Sam introduced us, he had a strange look in his eyes. I saw this but did not react. Not until it was too late.

Alan reminded me of a little weasel. He asked a lot of questions but didn't seem to have anything to offer me.

For the next few weeks, Alan called continuously. He kept saying he had people he wanted to introduce me to. I was open to all the help I could get in growing my small business. But when Alan introduced me to these people, I noticed they all had something in common: none of them could help me. This was because everyone Alan knew needed money more than I did.

Finally, I'd had it. Alan was wasting my time. One day I confronted him. I said, "Alan, everyone you've introduced me to needs help financially. How does this help me and my business?"

He replied, "It takes time, man. It will take time to find the right investors. Grant, don't give up on me yet."

MR. MUSTACHE

Alan invited me to an event being held at a well-known club in town. He called and said, "Meet me there at eight. There'll be a lot of people, including someone I want you to meet. Someone I'm sure can be helpful to you."

The club was happening. The room was packed with hot women, there was live music, the beautiful people were there in droves. Alan spotted me, and waved me over to a table.

He was sitting across from an older guy in a dark suit and tie with his hair slicked back. The guy had a well-groomed mustache. He wore an enormous pinky ring with diamonds in it.

Alan introduced us after I sat down. "Grant is in the skincare and cosmetics business."

"That's very interesting," Mr. Mustache replied. "Let's hear about it."

I described my business to Mr. Mustache. He paid close attention. Then he turned to Alan and said, "I need to talk with Grant alone. Can you come back in a little while?"

Alan said sure and walked off. I got up and followed him. I grabbed Alan's arm. "Where are you going? I don't know this guy from beans!"

Allen was stuttering, tripping over his own words. "Grant, Grant, I'll be back a in a little bit. Talk to him, talk to him, he wants to help you. He's waiting, don't make him wait!" Allen said and pulled away.

I sat down with Mr. Mustache. I asked him what he did for a living.

"I work for the state, doing various things," he replied.

"Very interesting. What kind of things?"

"Things I can't talk about."

That didn't sit well with me.

He leaned in and said, "I like your website, and your ideas. Your products, they look good. I went over all the ingredients." He nodded his approval.

Then he said something no business owner ever wants to hear.

"We'll work together to market your company. Then I'm going to take half your business. We're going to be partners, you and I."

I sat back in my seat. Huh? This was *not* in the game plan.

I put him off. "Let me think it over. After all, I don't know you," I replied.

"Okay, Grant. Go ahead and think. I'll give you a week to consider my offer. But I won't ask you again. We do the deal or else I will see to it that the state closes you down."

"I don't like being threatened," I replied. "So let me cut to the chase. My answer to you is no!"

A week later my business was closed down. My identity was stolen, and later on someone filed an outrageous tax return under the name of my corporation and tried to transfer money by wire from my account into their own. I reported all of this to the federal agencies that handle fraud and identity theft issues. I also purchased a product that protects your identity. And I bought an aluminum wallet for further protection.

I did not have any more of these kinds of problems.

I did a background check on Mr. Mustache. I found out he was playing both sides of the fence. He worked for the state, but he was also deeply involved in organized crime.

I later found out that Alan was an informant. He searched out corporations to plunder, companies looking for money, businesses big and small, illegal or legit. Alan too was playing both sides and was involved with crimes figures.

I also found out that my old acquaintance Sam knew all of this and set me up. Sam was an eight time loser in the business world, a convicted felon. He'd been in all sorts of trouble over the years. He saw my business venture had potential so he went for it. And he sold me out.

After that, I removed myself from social media.

CHAPTER 16

ALONE

I fell down and broke my foot at the gym due to wet floors in the locker room. My right leg was in a heavy cast from my toes up to my knee.

While recovering I stayed indoors. But one day I couldn't take it anymore. It was a beautiful morning, about seventy degrees and sunny, still brisk from a cool night.

I parked my car by the Intracoastal to watch the boats go by. The sun glistened, bouncing off the water as a sailboat eased past me, reggae music blasting from their stereo system. I had a cup of hazelnut coffee in hand, made just the way I like it, and a bottle of water to stay hydrated.

As I sat there, I tried to remain cheerful and not think about how alone I felt. After my accident, all of my so-called friends had abandoned me. All the women I liked did too. Nobody wanted to help me while I was laid up. One woman said, "Grant, call me when you can walk on both feet again."

Why would I? By that time, I wouldn't need her in my life anymore.

At least I still had my four-footed companion, man's best friend. And of course what was in my wallet. My father had learned this same lesson after he lost his real estate business and all his friends magically disappeared. When they could no longer take from you, people seemed to vanish as if by magic.

The coffee was warm and sweet. I sipped it and thought about the strangers I had met who were more compassionate toward me than the people I'd considered my friends. The kind of strangers who just seemed to slip through the cracks, suddenly there to help me in times of need.

The sun felt good on my skin. I needed to get out more.

The next day I made coffee, carefully maneuvering my scooter around the tiny condo kitchen. The sun was out and I needed to get back into it, rather than spend another day trapped in my shoebox home.

After coffee, I rode my scooter across the street to the local bagel shop. An oblivious patron let the entrance door close on me. The people in this town could be so rude and self-absorbed. They seemed callous, uncaring.

But I was trying to cheer myself up, so I ordered a lightly toasted bagel with a whisper of butter to take with me to the park.

The park was happening. People walked their dogs while others thronged around a live band playing fifties music. I sat in the sun and ate my bagel, trying not to feel so alone.

That night I struggled back into my car and drove to a local deli. I planned to order a large bowl of chicken noodle soup and a turkey Rueben on rye. But the hostess seated me at a table where I had nowhere to rest my leg. So I asked the manager to please square out the catty-corner table so I could fit my cast underneath.

The dinner got off to a bad start. Then the waitress appeared. She was polite, hospitable, and cheering. She served up my food hot, fast, and with a bright smile. She even gave a me a large glass of milk on the house. When I spoke, she looked into my eyes. It seemed like a miracle had happened.

I asked her name.

Brenda.

I asked Brenda where she was from. It was obvious she was not a local. She was too nice.

She asked me why I wanted to know. She had shiny brown hair and big brown eyes. She was petite and slender. She probably got hit on by customers all the time.

I said, "Since my accident, I've begun to see how people really are around here. Meeting you tonight has given me back my faith in humanity."

Brenda smiled. She said, "I'm from Cherry Hill, New Jersey."

I asked, "Is everyone from Cherry Hill, New Jersey, as nice as you are?"

She laughed and said, "I don't think so."

"So where do trees as nice and as beautiful as you grow? Because that's where I have to move to." It sounded like a line but I meant it.

Brenda laughed. "My parents taught me something called manners."

"There's a word that's not so popular around here."

Brenda smiled at me before she hurried off to the kitchen.

When she came back to check on me, I asked her to wrap up everything I couldn't finish. I figured this would make a good lunch for the next day. Brenda wrapped everything nicely, she was such a sweetheart.

I asked her to break a twenty, adding, "I want to give you a good tip for making my meal so enjoyable."

Brenda told me not to worry about it.

"But this is what you do for a living. I want to leave you a nice tip."

"I didn't do anything special. I'm just happy I could help you enjoy your dinner."

I replied, "I'll just have to take you out for coffee."

"My boyfriend would *not* like that."

I smiled and said, "Everyone has someone until someone better comes along." I handed her my business card. "Does your boyfriend know how lucky he is?"

She looked at me and paused, thinking. Then she responded, "I'm not sure."

"Well, that's not a good sign. Now you have my card, so use it!"

We smiled at one another.

On my way home I realized Brenda had helped me in so many ways. I felt less alone and my confidence had returned. There were nice people out there. I just had to get out and find them.

My depression lifted.

After that, it became easier for me to face the day as I healed from my injury.

THE OLYMPIAN

The next morning I checked the kitchen cabinets and found I had absolutely nothing to eat. So I headed to the grocery store.

While I was in the dairy aisle, I noticed a very nice looking woman talking to the store manager. She seemed to be inquiring about work. She was tanned and athletic looking with an impressive physique. The manager was curt, dismissive.

As I paid for my purchases at the register, I looked out the front window. The nice looking woman rode by on a blue bike. She stopped next door at a little luncheonette.

I hurried outside and put my groceries in the car. Then I followed her over to the restaurant.

She was inquiring again about work. Then she ordered a sandwich.

I thought maybe I could help her. I knew some of the owners and managers in the area from frequenting their establishments. I was attracted to her, and I wondered if I would like her as a person.

She sat at a small table by the entrance to keep an eye on her bike.

I purchased a bottle of water. As I passed her, I said, "Excuse me."

She looked up at me and said, "Hi."

She had given me an entrance so I stopped and said, "I was just in the grocery store and overheard you speaking with management to see if they needed help. It didn't seem to me they treated you very nicely."

She nodded. "Yes, I'm looking for a job. They told me to fill out an application and return it tomorrow." She rolled her eyes, which were large and brown and very pretty.

"I noticed they're hiring here. Have you asked them about a position?"

She shrugged. "Yes, but they don't have any shifts in the morning, just late afternoon into evening. That doesn't work for me. I'm going to apply at the coffee shop down the road, as well as the bagel place."

She extended her hand and said, "My name is Heather."

I replied, "I'm Grant. Nice to meet you."

She smiled. Her teeth were exceptionally white. She was really attractive.

I said, "Listen, I know a few of the business managers around here. Let me see if I can pull some strings. Give me a few days, maybe I can come up with something for you, Heather."

She smiled again and pulled a pen from her purse. Then she wrote down her number on a corner of her napkin.

When she handed it to me, she said, "So why do you want to help me?"

I shrugged. "I wanted to meet you, see what you're like. To be honest, I thought you looked like an interesting woman."

She looked down. "I used to be. I was an Olympian athlete."

I nodded. Of course, she was the real deal. I said, "There's nobody around here who looks as fit as you are. You certainly are a sight for sore eyes."

She grinned at me and invited me to sit down.

Heather told me she was raised on Long Island, not far from where I used to live. She had been a gymnast as a kid, and a swimmer. Then she trained to be a diver, and developed her skills. She'd made it all the way to the Olympics. Now divorced with two children, she was looking for work during their school hours.

We spent a pleasant hour together, talking.

It took me a few days but I found Heather a good job opportunity in a doctors' office where the pay would be generous. The office was located a block from her home. We met to go over her resume, which I had planned to submit to the doctors on her behalf.

As I was reviewing Heather's resume, she held up a hand. "I need to change a few things and update it."

Wasn't she supposed to do that before she started applying for work? I said, "Get that done ASAP."

She promised me she would. Her skin glowed in the afternoon sun. I was dying to ask her out.

A few days before my birthday, I decided to call Heather and ask if she had plans for the weekend. I was tired of being alone. I wanted to have someone in my life. That night, I left a message for her to call me.

I woke up to sunshine, another day closer to my birthday. Ugh.

While I was making coffee, Heather called. We made plans to meet and hang out. My day had suddenly brightened.

I met her at the local coffee shop. I arrived first and took a seat by the window. A few minutes later, Heather pulled up on her bike. She wore a pink shirt with skintight shorts revealing her fit figure.

We sat for a while and talked. Heather made steady eye contact with me. I was impressed with her intelligence, and her directness turned me on even more.

We made plans to meet up the next day, then kissed goodbye. I spent the remainder of the day in a positive frame of mind.

Heather emailed me the next morning with instructions on how to find her place. When I arrived, she hurried outside to my car. I took her to lunch at local restaurant. While we were eating sandwiches and chatting, her mother called. They started arguing so I went to the restroom.

When I came back to the table they were still fighting. Heather finally hung up on her mother, then apologized to me. I cracked a few jokes to loosen her up, and all was well again.

When we walked outside, Heather said, "Grant, I'm very selective about who I spend my time with, but there is something really special about you. I'd like to see more of you."

I was thrilled. "Thank you. I don't get many compliments, especially ones that are directed at me so sincerely."

She smiled and blushed.

We walked in the harsh sunshine toward the parking lot, talking about our families. She told me her father was in finance and owned many properties overseas. She didn't go into detail, but she seemed like she had been through a lot. She was beautiful and tough. I wanted to make her smile.

When I dropped her off, her family was just pulling up. They had come to visit her, like they did every Sunday.

Heather said, "I want to introduce you to my family."

I met her niece Maggie, who was cuter than cute, and her sister Jill. Then Heather introduced me to her mother. Everyone was nice and polite. But it was obvious she had not told them about me. I could feel their critiquing eyes trying to size me up.

The girls were taking bags from the car. Heather's mother bossed everyone around. She seemed controlling and overbearing. After meeting her, my heart went out to Heather.

I left after telling each of them how it had been a pleasure to meet them. Heather seemed giddy, happy to have introduced me to her family. She gave me a big hug and kiss goodbye before I drove off.

As I sped down the road in the warm sunshine, I felt great. I was very attracted to her and she seemed to really like me. But I was curious about her past. I needed to be careful before I became involved. What if her ex turned out to be the chief of police for some nearby town? I had learned the hard way not to dive in blindly.

I decided to run a background check on her. With a minimum amount of research, I found out Heather was related to the infamous mobster Mr. Whitewalls.

Oh no.

After dating a few women who had relatives with troublesome families, I had learned my lesson. I had experienced how protective and tightknit families can be. As much as I was physically attracted to her, I still didn't know her very well personally. Knowing she was related to the Whitewalls was enough, though. Enough for me not to want to pursue a relationship with Heather.

I liked my life simple and safe. I didn't want to walk on eggshells everywhere I went. I didn't want to feel restricted or threatened while protective eyes watched every move we made whenever we were out together.

A relationship with a woman from that kind of family was not a good idea if one was not from that same kind of background. Not unless one was completely out of one's mind.

Which I could be from time to time.

I might have allowed myself to get involved anyway, but Heather made the decision for me. The next day, she texted me. She said she would be busy with family all week. This was a surprise. We had made tentative plans for my birthday. She said her weekdays started at six thirty in the morning and she had a lot of responsibilities with the kids.

She was dumping me. Heather had suddenly changed her mind about me. I suspected the change of heart had to do with her mother.

My friend who worked at the doctors' office I sent Heather to told me she came in with an outdated resume and seemed distressed. This turned them off and they didn't hire her.

Heather blamed me for wasting her time with the job possibility. I was insulted. After all, I was not a therapist looking to help people resolve their crises in life. I was just looking for someone to spend my birthday with. Someone to have an honest relationship with. And that was not Heather.

Next!

A THREAT FROM THE PAST

Two months later, I received a collect call from Sing Sing. Yes, *that* Sing Sing, the maximum security state prison north of New York City. I didn't accept the charges, of course, because I didn't know anyone who had been sent there. After all, I didn't make it a habit to seek out and befriend convicts.

Whoever he was, the caller screamed over the operator as she was speaking to me. I heard him loud and clear after I rejected the call. He was threatening to kill me!

He called a few more times after that, always with the same message: "I'm going to kill you, and you won't see it coming!"

I replied "Obviously your employer didn't educate you on your subject. Two things you should know: There are a handful of alphabet agencies that have been keeping tabs on me for a very long time. In fact every phone has been monitored for decades. Even as we speak, this phone call has been triangulated and all of your information as well as all of your associate's info are being examined, right now, in real time. Your entire existence is going to be under a zoom microscope from now on, so, get ready for a shit storm!"

By the way, you can't kill me. He asked "Why is that?" I replied…

"Because… I'm already dead!"

He stopped calling.

A few weeks went by. Then I received a message from Melvin. Mr. Troublemaker. It had been two decades since we'd had contact. But I was easy to track down due to the Internet.

Melvin left a message directing me to call him back. He said it was important. But he was the last person in the world I would want to speak with, so of course I did not call him back.

I decided to do a background check on Melvin and the number he was calling from. It turned out to be his girlfriend's telephone number. And she had a job at Sing Sing; she was an administrator for the relocation program on the premises.

All the pieces fit together perfectly.

I once opened a fortune cookie and the fortune read: "Simplicity of character is the natural result of profound thought." I taped the fortune to my dresser when I was sixteen years old. The words remained etched in my mind throughout the decades that followed.

CHAPTER 17

THE FORMULA

A few months had gone by, my cast has been removed and I had been exercising frequently, tanning poolside, along with eating sensibly. I was in good shape when I bumped into Tom.

I had first met Tom at a health convention. We ran into each other many times after that. He was a spiritual guy, friendly and nice. I spoke to him on the phone every so often. I'd done a background check on Tom and he was clean as a whistle.

We were both guests at an extravagant party. The gleaming sports cars were parked out front. The women were dressed like a million dollars. The hors d'oeuvres kept coming, and the drinks flowed.

After we caught up on our lives, Tom introduced me to another man. Arnold was some type of biologist, so we talked about science. It was good to talk to someone who understood science. To some people, science is another language altogether.

I mentioned to Arnold that I had stayed in Bavaria. I explained about my treatments, and how the doctor was helping to restore my metabolism and resuscitate the mitochondria in the areas of my body that needed the most attention.

Arnold replied, "That's very interesting. I know of several scientists working to accomplish the same thing."

I was curious and asked for details.

"There's a group of scientists who have been trying to develop a formula that helps with mitochondria malfunction," he said.

"I'd love to learn more about what they're doing," I replied.

He nodded. "I'll give you a contact number. You can call and mention my name. Let's see what happens, shall we?"

I agreed. Why not?

The next day, I called the number Arnold had given me. I ended up on a three hour conference call. The researchers said they would send me a sample of the formula they were working on.

It took a few days for the package to arrive. The powder was white and had no odor. It was to be mixed into pure water, used in small amounts.

I enlisted the help of Scott. I went to his lab and we examined the product under a microscope. We read all the spec sheets, then studied the additional research they provided. The molecular structure under the microscope and the photos from their published papers were a match.

The formula seemed like the real thing. But would it work?

Only one way to find out. I would have to test the formula on myself.

The results were quite interesting. After using it once, I noticed my energy increased, everything around me seemed brighter, my outlook on life became more optimistic. I used it daily and I felt good. Better, but not perfect. In fact, there was something vital missing.

What was it that was missing, I asked myself. It was like an eighty percent complete jigsaw puzzle that needed that missing twenty percent to make it whole.

I consulted with Scott, figuring he might know what was needed, but I hit a brick wall. Scott didn't know what could be missing.

There was only one person I knew who might be able to help. Dr. Siegfried.

I placed a long-distance call to Bavaria. The doctor answered my call and I explained everything in great detail.

He replied, "My boy, I know what the formula is missing. But I will only tell you if you will promise to come visit us here in Bavaria. Can you come within the next few weeks?"

He said they missed me. Ursula missed me.

That was nice to know. I said, "I promise I'll be back in a few weeks."

"Very good! When you come, make sure to bring some of this formula you speak of."

"Of course, Dr. Siegfried. After all, you need to see this more than anyone else I know."

He laughed and said, "True!"

"So, what do you think may be missing in the formula?"

"My boy, when the metabolism slows down, the mitochondria start to malfunction and there is a buildup of excess hydrogen which does not allow oxygen to penetrate any of the cells properly, thus inhibiting cellular respiration."

"What should I do?" I asked.

"It's so easy to resolve," Dr. Siegfried replied. "My mentor was the apprentice for one of the most famous cell physiologists in the world. He figured out how to resolve this issue ninety years ago in Berlin."

Dr. Siegfried then proceeded to tell me what to do, how to formulate a simple concoction to go with the formula I had been taking.

I obtained most of the supplies I needed from the local grocery store and my friend's garden. I then combined Dr. Siegfried's concoction with the scientists' formula. I began taking it in small doses right away.

The results were nothing less than miraculous. After ingesting this combination, the new enhanced formula, I felt awesome. The energy and clarity was incredible. It was like being a kid again, but with an additional boost of testosterone.

As the days progressed, so did my feeling of well-being. The stuff worked miracles.

HERMAN

A few days later, I was standing in front of Len's house. He was out of town so I had told him I'd check on things for him and water the plants. I spotted a baby gecko on the sidewalk. It had a bump on its head and appeared to be deteriorating. Its neck was stuck in a strange position. I studied the little guy for a while. I didn't know what I could do to help.

Then the light bulb went on inside my head. The formula!

I relocated the gecko to some fresh soil under a lemon tree that had been planted in a giant ceramic pot. The pot was full of potting soil rich in nutrients. The soil had minerals and moss. This could be the gecko's little island.

The gecko was on his back, he looked bad. I mixed up small batch of the formula, and I grabbed my camera. I obtained some basil from my friend's garden, along with some earthworms. I made a concoction with ground up worms, crushed basil, and the formula.

In Len's bathroom, I found a medicine dropper I could use to drip-feed the baby gecko. As I prepared to feed him, I decided to name him Herman.

I plunged the dropper in the special formula, then tried to entice Herman to eat. It wasn't easy. My first attempts failed. I dripped some onto the bump on his head, thinking at least I could try to heal that up.

The formula dripped down the side of his tiny head. Some dripped into his mouth and he must have decided he liked it. Suddenly he opened his mouth wide. As if asking for more.

I filled up the dropper. Herman's mouth opened very wide, and I squeezed the formula into his mouth. I watched him digesting it as his body began to assimilate the nutrients. His belly was clear, and transparent to some degree. It was wonderful to see him thriving on the formula he had quickly acquired a taste for.

After he was done eating, his body started to react. He began to shake vigorously, then quieted; this happened several times. Then he looked up at me. We stared at one another. He settled back down, closed his eyes and took a nap.

The next morning, Herman was up bright and early. When I arrived on the patio, he looked like he was waiting for me. His neck seemed to have straightened out. He was up on his feet, acting energetic and alert. He came close to the camera, jumped on my finger, then leaped back on the soil around the lemon tree.

This was unusual behavior for a gecko. I petted his back and head as he walked closer to the camera, looking right into the lens. I fed him more formula, to which he responded enthusiastically.

Within three days, the bump on his head was completely gone. Herman must have felt all better because, after four days of treatment with the formula, he took off. When I went to see him on his little island, he was gone.

I was happy for him and glad I had captured the events on camera. Otherwise, nobody would have believed I had a friendship with an ailing gecko named Herman.

BEVERLY

I wanted to share the story with someone. It was so cool, how the little gecko had recovered his health.

One afternoon my neighbor came over. Beverly was an elderly widow, warm and motherly. We had coffee together on occasion.

After I showed her the video footage, she was stunned. She said it was as if the lizard had healed right before her eyes.

She said, "Grant, *I* want to experience what that little creature did. I want to feel young again. I want to feel youthful and full of energy. Could you make me a batch of your formula so I can try it too?"

I said, "Why not?"

I smiled at her tired, wrinkled face. Her eyes were red and watery, her shoulders stooped. She smiled weakly and said in a tiny voice, "Thank you."

I set up at my laboratory workstation, which doubled as my kitchen table, and went to work. I mixed my formula with some very special water that I had treated in a unique way.

After studying the work of some of the greatest scientists of our time, I was able piece together their findings and use my new-found knowledge to manipulate pure water. I used the special water I had made as the base for the enhanced formula. I felt so wonderful from drinking it myself that the only thing I could compare it to was the fountain of youth.

How splendid it was to study the masters in order to acquire their knowledge and use it in a recipe! How amazing to sit back and savor one of the finest moments in your life when a major accomplishment had been successfully achieved.

Beverly drank down the glass of formula I handed her and smiled at me. I gave her a bottle and told her to take a small amount daily.

After weeks of ingesting my formula on a regular basis, my neighbor's face was transformed. The pasty, haunted look had completely vanished. There was color in her cheeks. Her eyes were clear and they sparkled. She looked full of life and enthusiasm. She was performing tasks around the house she had been avoiding for years due to lack of strength and energy. Her listlessness had dissolved.

One day I ran into Beverly in the hall. She said in a buoyant voice, "Grant, now I know how Herman feels!" She smiled at me with delight. "He must love you for helping him."

I asked her how she felt.

Beverly skipped down the hall between our apartments and jogged back. She said, "It's amazing! This is the best I've felt in the longest time. In fact, I haven't felt this energetic since I was twenty-one years old and took my first trip to Miami. I stayed at a wonderful hotel right on the beach and my life felt stress-free. It was like I lived in a tropical dream. That's how this stuff of yours is making me feel."

Then she laughed until tears of joy rolled down her soft cheeks.

I grinned. How cool!

She said, "Whatever you put in there, don't change the formula. Keep everything the way it is because you got it right. I hope you wrote everything down on paper and put it somewhere safe."

SHEILA

The next day I called Dr. Siegfried and told him everything. "You can see the difference the formula makes, and in no time at all. Imagine how many people, how many animals we could help with this stuff!"

Dr. Siegfried said, "I am curious to look at the formulation, Grant."

I told him, "When you look at the chemical composition and the molecular structure, I'm sure you'll be able to make it into an even more effective formulation."

"We'll see, my boy. But we need you here."

I said, "Good news. I've purchased a one-way ticket. I leave from Miami on Thursday night. I should be there sometime on Saturday."

Dr. Siegfried said, "Send me your flight information and I will have a car waiting for you."

"Thank you, Dr. Siegfried. I'm excited to see you. And to see everyone."

I meant Ursula.

That evening after dinner, I went to the condo sauna. The heat felt good on my skin. The amber wood coupled with the eucalyptus spray I had misted smelled wonderful. I poured cold water over the hot rocks and the sizzling sound relaxed me. As the moist heat enveloped the room, it gave me a feeling of deep comfort. My hair felt hot, my muscles loose and limp.

When I left the sauna, I slipped into the steaming Jacuzzi. The water was one hundred and forty degrees and the jets were bubbling against the areas of my body that needed attention. Muscle knots were dissolving, melting away like ice on a sunny day in Florida. As those bubbles enveloped me, I began to feel more and more relaxed. I could feel my heart beating rhythmically in my chest.

This caused my mind to unwind and loosen. I felt peaceful and comfortable in every way.

I began to daydream about Herman. I felt so good about helping him. He was able to heal up so quickly. It had been my first experience connecting with a lizard. When he looked up into my eyes, there was an understanding there beyond words.

My mind wandered to Dr. Siegfried and what a special, warm, and wonderful person he was. I felt excited about showing him the formula. I had a strong longing to be back on the doctor's estate. It felt like home there, and like I was family.

In a pleasant daze, I lifted myself out of the tub and went back to my condo to take a shower. The hot water seeped into my muscles. The soap I was using was an organic bar Mielle had given me, along with all-natural shampoo and conditioner. The ingredients were pure. Using the products made me feel as though I was bathing in French Polynesia or some other exotic island untouched by man and still natural and pure. I felt whisked away as I lathered up my body and stood under the hot, steaming shower. This was my little island.

When I shut off the shower, I towel dried my body. I felt incredibly clean and refreshed.

I put on a terrycloth robe and got ready to go to bed.

There was a knock at my door. I peered out the peephole. Sheila?

I opened the door. Sheila.

A beautiful dark-haired dancer, Sheila was a new friend. I had been seeing her for only a few months.

This was a nice surprise.

She came in and gave me a hug. "You smell good, Grant. Were you going to bed?"

"I was about to," I replied.

"Do you mind if I join you?" she asked with a wide smile.

"Please. Make yourself at home," I replied.

As we slipped under the satin sheets together, Sheila winked at me. Then she turned off the lamp by the bed.

The rest, as they say, is history.

CHAPTER 18

LEN AND THE FORMULA

The next morning Sheila left for work and I went into the kitchen to make myself some breakfast. Before I even got started on the coffee, Len called. He was back in town and wanted to hang out.

"I know this cool place we can go for breakfast," he told me.

I didn't want to cook anything so I said, "Okay, let's go."

Len picked me up in his cherry red sports car and we drove to Bal Harbour, a ritzy shopping area. Len pulled in under the neon sign that said Wolfie's Rascal House. The establishment had been there for more than fifty years. "A landmark," Len said when he parked the car in the crowded lot.

The décor was Miami modern. The hostess seated us in a comfortable booth. The waitress asked, "Coffee?"

We both nodded, said thanks in unison, then looked at each other and laughed.

I said, "Listen, I'm leaving to go back to Bavaria in a few days."

"Why? Seems like you don't need the treatments anymore. You look so healthy."

"Business and pleasure," I told him with a wink.

"Speaking of that, I have something I want to talk to you about," he said. "I can't tell you here, though; we need to go somewhere more private. I'll tell you when we get back in the car. We can drive up A1A."

I thought that sounded great, so we ate and talked of other things.

After breakfast we drove up the coast on A1A, admiring the view of the aqua ocean and glimpses of the smooth blue Intracoastal. It was a gorgeous day, cloudless and not too hot. Everything felt right. I had a wonderful sense of well-being which I attributed to the night before.

After a while I said, "So, what's on your mind?"

"If I tell you, you can't tell anyone else. Do you promise?"

"Of course," I said.

"Grant, my Uncle Lenny passed away."

"I'm sorry to hear that," I replied.

"I really liked him a lot."

"I know what that feels like. If there's anything I can do, let me know."

He said, "Well, there is something you can help me with."

"What?"

"See, I want to feel better and I know you studied nutrition. You fixed your own health. You're doing great now. So can you help me with mine? See, my uncle left me some serious money. So, well, I could pay you…" He gave me a beseeching look.

"Okay, I think I might be able to help you in that department." I told him about the formula, about my response to it, about Herman and Beverly. Then I told him about the video I had of Herman's recovery.

He slammed on his brakes. "You have all this on video?"

I nodded.

"I want to see it as soon as possible!"

"Maybe when you're ready to do what it takes to feel better," I said. He would need to make a commitment. Len was a party animal, he liked to laze around and have fun.

"Grant, I've been ready since last year! You *have* to show me the video and tell me *everything*! I can't believe you didn't tell me all of this before," he said. "Next time you have a secret like this and you don't tell me, I'm going to have that fitness chick you liked come over and kick your ass!"

I laughed. Some threat.

Len demonstrated the aerodynamics of his sports car, speeding all the way back to my condo.

When we arrived, I made us a pot of coffee. Len was antsy, pacing around the tiny living room. He kept saying, "Hurry up and get the video ready!"

I couldn't stop laughing. But I was excited too. He seemed so into it. This reassured me. I might have done something important. Maybe the video and the formula could help others and impact health on a grand scale.

We both sat down with our coffee to watch the video.

After, Len turned to me and said in a hushed voice, "That is the most amazing thing I have ever seen. Wow!"

I replied, "Just think, it all began at *your* front door."

Len begged, "Please, Grant, give me some of that formula? I want to drink some right now!"

"Okay, but you can't tell anyone," I said. "The formula is still in development."

"Okay, it'll stay our secret."

I took a small bottle of the formula out of my pocket and handed it to him.

Len gaped and said, "You had the formula in your pocket this whole time?"

I smiled and said yeah.

He looked as though he went to pull the hair out of his head. "You tell me about this amazing formula, this incredible discovery, this huge secret. And you've had it in your pocket the whole *time*?" He shook his head in wonder.

I poured some formula in a water glass. I added glacial water, then handed it to him.

He said, "So will I really feel like myself again?"

I nodded. "Absolutely."

He drank it down. When he asked to stay over I said sure.

The next day, Len was up early. He made breakfast for us. "I think I'm beginning to feel better," he said, pouring coffee.

"You're going to start feeling better and better. That's how this stuff works," I promised. I sent him home with a small bottle. No charge.

I was packed to go back to Bavaria. Len came by to say goodbye and to tell me he felt great. "I feel better now than I can ever recall," he said with a big smile.

I made up another batch of the formula for Len, enough so he could take it daily while I was away. I told him not to waste any. The formula was expensive to produce.

He nodded. "Maybe I can help out with that. Grant, my uncle left me a small fortune. I already know I'm going to take this formula on a regular basis so maybe I can help fund production. After all, it's the only thing that makes me feel good."

That sounded like a good plan to me. I wasn't selling the stuff so I would need money to make it in the kind of quantities I'd need to bring it to market. Once the formula was perfected, that is.

I said, "Okay. And I know what you mean. The formula really makes me feel alive, too."

Len offered to drive me to the airport the next day. "You don't have to take a taxi, I'll drive you," he said.

Thursday morning arrived and the day was gorgeous. I went for a walk by the ocean. The sea air was thick and clean. It felt good to take long deep breaths. The waves rolled in one after the other as the sandpipers ran along the shoreline. The seagulls were stalking fish for breakfast while the bright sun rose above the ocean as if emerging out of the sea. The deep red sun gradually turned a bright orange.

People walked by and said hello. I smiled and said good morning as we passed one another. A girl was swimming in the turquoise ocean. Pelicans flew in formation overhead.

I found a bench where I could sit to wipe the sand off my feet. Across the street was a luncheonette I had heard served a nice breakfast. I was hungry after the long walk. I decided to stop in for a bite to eat.

A beautiful waitress came over to the table I had chosen. She smiled and said good morning. I replied in the same fashion and placed my order. Then I asked "What's your name?"

"Lee" she replied.

"Lee, with a smile as nice as yours, how could I ever have another waitress?" She laughed.

I said, "I mean it. I guess I'm just going to have to sweep you off your feet and make you my wife."

Lee laughed again and said, "Let me go get your eggs before they're cold. I want them to be hot for you."

"You are the best!"

She smiled and hurried off to the kitchen. When she came back, my eggs were steaming hot, along with the cup of coffee she poured for me.

When I asked her where she was from, she replied, "Arkansas."

I said, "They're sure doing something right in Arkansas."

"What do you mean?"

"If there were more women like you in the world, this planet would be a much sweeter place to live."

She laughed. "Well, thank you. Are you always so nice to people you've just met?"

I shrugged. "This happens on the rare occasions when a certain someone piques my interest."

Lee blushed and said, "I better tend to the other customers before they get cranky."

We both laughed.

The eggs were delicious. I would have to return after my trip. I would come back to see Lee and enjoy the food.

When I paid my check, I thanked her. She gave me a beautiful smile in return. The perfect sendoff for my trip to Bavaria.

CHAPTER 19

BACK TO BAVARIA

I knew it would be a long flight, so I used the restroom before we took off. When I came back to my assigned seat, I made myself comfortable, stretching out my legs as I reclined. There was a selection of movies to watch and plenty of legroom in first class.

The pilot's voice came over the loudspeaker. "We are ready to depart the gate. Please, take your seats and put your seatbelt on."

We had clearance to proceed for takeoff, so the plane started moving slowly down the runway. I sat there strapped into my seat, and the plane moved faster and faster. I could feel my body being pinned back. My muscles grew hard as the pure force and power of the plane thrust us forward, then up and into the air. My heart began to race as the plane climbed higher and higher in the sky.

We eventually evened out. Then I could take a deep breath and sigh in relief as my body began to relax. I figured it would be smooth sailing all the way to Europe.

I stretched out for a nap. I sank back into my seat and let my mind go as I gradually drifted off to sleep.

I had the most remarkable dream.

I was sleeping in Ursula's bed and it felt so wonderful. It felt wonderful to feel so wonderful again. But it felt even more wonderful than before because this time I was in the arms of someone who loved me for who I was. This provided me with a secure reassurance that made me feel whole. The feeling enriched my life and made everything seem worthwhile. Ursula and I were bonded together, our energies united, making us a complete unit. We were full of compassion, love, empathy, and sincerity. I felt a glowing warmth that connected our two hearts, our two souls, and our two minds, making us one.

The sun was just coming up. As it peeked through the window, our bodies locked together. I hugged her tight and…

Ding, ding, ding!

An alarm clock? It didn't sound like any alarm clock I'd heard before.

"Please fasten your seatbelts for landing."

I woke up with a start. I was dreaming, and the sun was just rising in Europe.

I strapped in as we began to descend for the landing. We landed perfectly, and here I was, back in Germany.

Even as I walked through the bustling airport, I could still feel the warm, loving, tender emotions from my dream. They had lingered, strong yet surreal.

"Grant!"

I turned around and there she was. Ursula. She looked as beautiful as I remembered. She ran over to me, and as we hugged, then kissed passionately.

"I think you missed me," she said with a giggle.

"I have been waiting to hold you like this. In fact, on the plane I had the most amazing dream about us. It was so surreal, and so clear, I really thought I was with you."

Ursula put a hand on my face. "Where were we in your dream?"

"In your bed, of course. Under those satin sheets, embracing each other. And as our breathing became more shallow, relaxed, and in sync, I felt your love for me like never before. This made me have deeper and stronger feelings for you."

Her eyes glowed.

I said, "There was a certain understanding between us. It was something words can't describe. Like a vibration that locked us together in a kind of harmony that made my life feel whole."

Ursula began to cry. "Grant, I had a dream like that too! It's like we dreamed the same dream last night!"

I nodded. Strange, yet not so strange. "Our souls united last night, because that's how strong our love is."

Ursula wiped away her tears and said, "I think you're right. Oh, Grant."

I kissed her passionately again, then put my arm around her as we walked toward the Town Car. The driver opened the door for us.

As we drove to the doctor's estate, I wrapped my arm around Ursula. We rode in comfortable silence, both of us looking out the windows at the lush landscape. The foothills were all around us, the trees thick and dark green, while the mountain tops glistened white, covered in thick snow. I opened my window so we could hear the icicles cracking, the wind blowing through the trees. The air was crisp and the fragrance of cedar filled the air.

As we drove a winding road over some steep hills, I could see Dr. Siegfried's estate in the distance. The place looked magnificent. I was happy to be back.

When we arrived, Dr. Siegfried was waiting in the living room, looking out the window at our approach. He looked older but glowing with good health.

As we came through the door, I heard the doctor's deep voice. "Angus, Grant and Ursula have arrived. Please help Grant with his bags."

"Right away," Angus replied and he appeared in the vestibule. He asked me, "Did you have a pleasant trip, sir?"

"The flight was smooth and the trip was perfect, thank you," I replied.

Angus grabbed my luggage and took it up the stairs to my quarters.

"My boy, where are you?" Dr. Siegfried called. He was sitting in front of the fireplace. He stood up and smiled when I came in the room. "Grant, how good to see you again! Here, sit down, please. You had a long flight. Come in and relax. We have a lot to talk about. I want to know all about your time in Florida."

I sat down. The fire roared, the intense heat warming me all over.

"Would you like some of our hot cocoa?"

I nodded enthusiastically. "Yes, please."

Dr. Siegfried called to Angus. "Please make two cups of hot cocoa for Grant and myself. With some of that fresh whipped cream that you make so well."

Angus said, "Right away, sir," and left the room smiling.

"Grant, it's going to take you a few days to adapt to the time difference."

"Yes, I know, but that's all right. I'm just happy to be here."

"It looks like you missed us. And, by the way you're looking out the window at Ursula, I would guess you missed her quite a bit," Dr. Siegfried said.

I laughed quietly. "More than I realized," I admitted.

"That's very good, Grant. You're part of our family now, so you belong here with us."

We sipped our delicious cocoa while I told him about Florida. The cool blue ocean, the palm trees, the hot sand, the people. My eyes were getting heavy and Dr. Siegfried noticed.

"Grant, we can talk more later. I have some things to do, and you must rest. Go ahead upstairs. You can unpack and make yourself at home."

I went up to my quarters and unpacked my belongings. Then I lay down on the big soft bed and drifted off to sleep.

When I woke up, I felt refreshed. I opened my bag to the side compartment where I had packed several vials of the formula. I took one vial and hurried downstairs to find Dr. Siegfried.

He was in his laboratory. As soon as I showed him the vial, he got ready to perform a thorough evaluation and chemical analysis. I watched as he began a series of tests. He tested the surface tension. He also used something called a spectrometer as well as microscopy to study the chemical composition and structural components. After a while, I left him to his work and went to find Ursula.

The tests went on for days. Finally, the analysis was complete to Dr. Siegfried's satisfaction.

He invited me to the lab. When I arrived, Dr. Siegfried said, "The formula is quite impressive. The tests show that everything you told me on the phone was accurate. The chemical composition is exact. I have never come across a formulation like this in all my years in research. This formula is a true age-defying, cellular rejuvenating, self-healing medicine. If it works as you've described, it's an absolute miracle!"

I smiled, embarrassed and pleased.

"I would like to try some myself, to feel the effects of taking the formula," he said.

I nodded. "Certainly, Dr. Siegfried."

I mixed him a dose using the glacial water he had on hand. I poured the water into a large glass, measured out a full teaspoon of the formula, and added it to the water. I mixed it vigorously before handing it to him.

"To our health and preservation," Dr. Siegfried said. Then he drank down the elixir.

He took additional doses of the formula for several days.

One afternoon he called me into the lab. "Grant, you were right. This stuff works. I feel invigorated, rejuvenated, and just plain wonderful. I think we have something truly remarkable here. Now you need to show me the video you made of the lizard, the one you fed the formula to."

"Okay, let me set things up so we can watch it."

"I have to say, Grant, this is the most riveted I have been by anything in a long time. The potential for this formula is absolutely mindboggling."

I smiled. I had to agree. "I'm glad you're excited. If you're behind the formula, then I can be sure it's good."

I set up the video, connecting to a large flat screen television the doctor used for dark field microscopy. We both sat down in front of the screen and I turned on the video, which I had edited to make as clear as possible.

Dr. Siegfried said, "My goodness, it looks as though the gecko has a contusion on the top of the head."

I replied, "Yes, that's why you see me placing drops of the formula on the contusion, to help Herman heal and recover. As you can see, the formula dripped down from there and went into his mouth."

"Yes, I see that."

"Now watch closely. You can see how he opens his mouth, wider and wider, and he reaches for the dropper, for me to feed him more of the formula. As he swallows the formula, his belly contracts and expands. See that? Look how he opens his mouth as if to say, *more, I want more.*"

When he saw Herman's body shake, Dr. Siegfried said, "The gecko needed this formula, my boy! His body went into shock from ingesting so much nutrition, the kind of nutrients that he so desperately needed. You helped give him his life back, Grant."

I shrugged. "I'm happy that I had access to something special so I could do this for him. Herman is innocent, like most creatures. His only motives were to feel better, to eat, to drink, to feel the sunshine, breathe fresh air, and have a sense of unity, compassion, and love."

"Don't we all want the same?" Dr. Siegfried asked.

"Yes, we do."

"In Hebrew, what you have done is called a mitzvah."

I laughed. "How do you even know the term?" I asked him.

"I have many Jewish friends, people I befriended during the war while I was guiding them to freedom. When they wrote to me later, after they'd escaped Nazi Germany, they taught me the terminology."

I was impressed. The man was a hero.

We watched as Herman made a complete recovery. He seemed as though he was smiling at me through the camera lens. He moved closer and closer so I could pet him.

"The next day, he was gone," I told the doctor. "Off to freedom and to explore the beauty of South Florida."

"Grant, that is just the most remarkable film. You should be proud of yourself. Your compassion, love, and affection for all living creatures shines through in this film you made," Dr. Siegfried said quietly. He sounded impressed.

"Thank you, I appreciate that," I replied.

"You must show the film to Ursula."

That night I shared the video with her. Ursula looked at me with an expression I interpreted as deep love and respect. I think she was more in love with me after that.

The next day, Ursula took me sightseeing. We visited a historical castle. The architecture was extraordinary, like something right out of every fairytale ever told. We wandered down long stone halls and up and down curving staircases. The view of the thick dark forest was amazing.

I kept thinking how it felt so surreal. It seemed to me that a castle like that was what dreams were made of.

When we arrived back at the doctor's estate, I made reservations for us to go to a luxury spa in Switzerland. The world renowned hotel was located high in the Alps, where the air was thin and the mountains vast and imposing.

CHAPTER 20

MAUI TO MIAMI

After spending a few days at the fancy spa in Switzerland, we were relaxed and happy. I made more reservations and we flew to Hawaii. My old friend Fred lived in Maui, where he had refurbished an old barn, turning it into a rustic bed-and-breakfast.

The flight to Hawaii was beautiful, a smooth ride the whole way there.

Upon landing, we exited into the air-conditioned terminal. We were greeted by throngs of lovely Hawaiian women. They handed us fresh flower leis that smelled exquisite. In fact, the main island smelled wonderful. The air was clean and warm, full of the aromas of fresh earth, sea water, and blooming tropical plants.

Fred stood outside, waiting for us. I introduced Ursula while he was gathering up our bags with his assistant Paul.

"How was the flight?" Fred asked.

Ursula and I replied, "Great!"

Paul drove us in their Jeep to the seaplane we would take to Maui. The island was gorgeous, lush and green with exotic flowers everywhere.

We boarded the seaplane, and flew out over the Pacific. I watched a school of dolphins playing and swimming in the clear water below us. Ursula laughed and grabbed my arm in excitement.

When we landed in Maui, it was like paradise. We wandered the balmy beach and tried a variety of local foods, big juicy fruits I had never eaten before. The sun was hot, the sky cloudless.

That evening there was a fire dance show at the restaurant where we went to dinner. The most beautiful deep orange sunset was clearly visible from our table.

Ursula leaned over to whisper in my ear. "Grant, this is like the movies I've seen of Hawaii."

I whispered back, "Yes, but the difference is, we're in it!" I grabbed her hand and kissed it, then kissed her lips.

After dinner, we strolled the beach, holding hands. We laughed at a turtle that ducked into the water, and then stuck out its head to peer at us.

When we got back to the bed-and-breakfast, Fred was sitting with his wife on the front porch.

"Grant, Ursula, you haven't had the pleasure of meeting my wife Camille."

We introduced ourselves. Camille was lovely, and instantly hospitable. "Would you care for some of our special homemade strawberry lemonade?" she asked.

We said yes please, so she left for the kitchen.

She returned with two large icy mugs.

"Thank you," I said to Camille. "Fred, this island is magical. Now I understand why you live here."

He smiled and said, "You're both welcome here anytime."

"Thanks," I replied.

We sipped the delicious lemonade and chatted for a while.

Finally I said, "Ursula and I are going to retire for the evening. We'll see you in the morning."

Fred and Camille said goodnight as we left for our room.

In the king size bed, I lay beside Ursula as she slept. I could smell the fresh orchids and hear the relaxing sound of the ocean as wave after wave came pounding to the shore.

That night I had the most lucid dream. I was at my mother's condominium. I heard this noise: *Clunk, drag, clunk, drag*, then a loud *good morning!* In the dream I asked myself *where am I and how did I get here?* I made myself some hazelnut coffee and it smelled wonderful. I began to sip my coffee and it tasted amazing. Then, I felt something wet on my arm.

When I looked down, Scotty was licking me. The dog was wagging his tail and smiling! As I petted him, his hair felt long, much too long for a dog. Something was wrong.

Then I heard, *Grant, Grant!* It didn't sound like my mother's voice. Too young and...

I opened my eyes. Ursula was smiling at me, kissing my arm. Then she kissed my lips gently.

"Ursula, I was just dreaming. It was so real! I thought I was in Florida."

"You're not, you're here with me in beautiful Maui."

"Thank goodness," I replied.

"Fred left us some really good hazelnut coffee. He put it outside our door."

"How did Fred know I like hazelnut coffee?"

Ursula winked. "I told him. So he called a friend who supplies most of the island with every kind of coffee imaginable, from everywhere."

"Fred is something else," I replied.

I pulled Ursula to me and kissed her. We were both laughing as I led her to the shower.

We spent a wonderful day together at the beach and wandering around the island.

That evening, Ursula made it clear she wanted to get married. If we were to continue the relationship, she wanted us to wed.

I told her, "I need time to give this some serious thought."

She replied, "You need time? I'll give you all the time you need to figure things out. Time you can spend *by yourself.*"

"What does that mean?"

"It means I'm taking the next flight home to Europe," she said. "You need time to think things over, and that's precisely what I'm going to give you. Take all the time you need. Take the rest of your life," she said in a loud voice.

Then she locked herself in the bathroom.

In the morning she packed her things and left. Fred and Camille didn't know what to say, but they attempted to be supportive and comforting. I was bereft.

I called Len that evening. I explained what had happened with Ursula and told him I'd be flying back to Florida in the morning.

Len said, "I'll be at the airport waiting for you, bro. You can stay at my place as long as you need to."

I said, "Len, thanks for being there for me."

He replied, "No problem, that's what friends are for. I'll see you tomorrow."

I packed my belongings and tried to get some sleep. In the morning, it was hot and sunny so I went for a swim in the ocean. The water was brisk and clean.

After I dried off, Fred was waiting on the porch with Camille. He said, "Grant, you can stay here for a while if you'd like. Stay as long as you wish."

I replied, "Thank you for being so nice, but I really need to take care of some things back home."

They drove me to the seaplane which would take me back to the mainland.

As I climbed out of the van, Fred said, "Don't be a stranger. If you ever need to get away, we're here for you. Our home is your home."

Camille said, "We'd love to have you stay longer next time."

I thanked them again, hugged them both goodbye, then boarded the seaplane.

LEN, LEVY AND LESTER

The ride was choppy but fun. When I arrived on the Big Island, the shuttle took me to the airport. I waited for about an hour, then boarded the plane to Florida. It was a long flight, but smooth sailing all the way.

I arrived in Miami right on time. Len was waiting for me in the baggage claim area. He gave me a big hug, then I followed him out to the parking lot. I put my things in the trunk of his shiny little sports car.

We drove through the humid night. Len pulled into the lot of a nice little restaurant that had just opened. The bistro was beautiful inside and the prices were surprisingly reasonable. We sat at a table in the back.

We ordered drinks and appetizers. I had serious jetlag and felt wired from lack of sleep. My emotions were all over the place.

After we talked about what had happened with Ursula, I blurted, "I'm thinking about writing a book."

Len raised one eyebrow. He asked, "Fiction or nonfiction?"

When I said I was thinking about writing about my life, Len nodded. He asked, "Will I be in the book?"

"Yes. But I'll write it like a novel, one that is based on events that really happened to me."

He nodded again, and then smiled. "Grant that sounds really interesting. What made you decide to write a book?"

I thought about it. The idea had popped fully formed into my head. So what *had* given me the urge to write about my life?

I said, "Many people I met over the years have been so interesting. Some were odd, or even threatening. But it's been fascinating knowing these characters. I've been through a lot in my life, and I'd like to share that with others."

He looked at me and sipped his ice water. "Tell me what you've been through that you haven't told me about. Is there something you haven't shared with me?"

I said, "I can't tell you everything right now."

"How come?"

"It will all be in my book," I replied.

He gave me a curious look, and then shrugged. "Okay, I understand. So just tell me the things you don't think you'll put in your book."

We both laughed.

I said, "I just came off a very long flight. Cut me some slack, Len." I changed the subject. "So how's your energy level?"

Len smiled. "I was just going to ask you if you can get me—"

I interrupted him. "More of the formula?"

We laughed.

Len said, "I've been feeling so good!"

We finished our drinks, then Len drove us back to his place. I lugged my suitcase upstairs, happy to be back in my old room again. I was tired, so I hit the sack early.

The next morning, I woke up refreshed, ready for a hot breakfast. After I made myself some coffee, I called my friend Tom. "I'm back in town."

He said, "Great! Let's get together tomorrow."

"Okay. Where do you want to meet?"

Tom laughed. "Where my friends and I always meet on Tuesdays. Everyone has been asking for you. I know they would love to see you."

Tom was a bit older than I was, so his friends were too, but they were nice folks. I attended their weekly meetings once in a while. But it had been a while.

I replied, "That sounds great."

Tom said, "Meet us at the diner at six. I'll see you then."

When I met up with Tom and his friends at the diner, there were a couple of new faces. Levy introduced himself. He struck me as a very strange individual. He seemed secretive, and constantly laughed at his own private jokes. It was as if he had some kind of agenda. I could tell this by the way he looked at me, his body language told me everything I needed to know. My gut feeling was there was something very wrong with him.

This was also true of his friend Lester. His name wasn't really Lester, I never learned his real name. But boy, the guy loved to talk. He took center stage at the round table, and told us all about the many adventures he'd had on his travels around the world. Lester was a windbag but absolutely fascinating to listen to. His knowledge on a variety of subjects was outstanding. I could ask him a question and Lester would have knowledge on that subject, along with an answer. He was self-centered and domineering, but impressive.

One of the ladies at the table got a word in edgewise and asked, "What is it that you do for a living?"

Lester hesitated, then said something vague, not answering her directly.

She came back with, "Well, who is it you work for?"

Everyone at our table turned to Lester, waiting to hear his answer.

He shrugged. "I worked for the government for many years, but that's about as much as I can tell you. I've traveled all over the world, and I've met every kind of person from all walks of life from almost everywhere. I speak seven different languages, and have been studying human behavior my whole life."

Lester went on about his time in Egypt, his stay in rural France, and his second home in Belgium. It seemed to me he might have studied theology by the way he spoke.

I asked him about that and he smiled at me.

"Yes! For many years. I needed to know more about different religious beliefs, as well as ceremonial customs and traditions. I learned about the theologies of peoples from the middle east into northern Africa. So when I visit these countries, I can communicate with the people more effectively."

Lester began explaining various dogmas to the group. People tuned out, and turned away to chat with one another. The information was complicated and intense, but I found it fascinating.

The conversation with the group became a conversation between just Lester and I, while everyone else at the table talked among themselves.

When Lester went to the restroom, I apologized to everyone else for ignoring them. They said they understood. When he had joined the group the week before, someone said, he had so much to talk about he monopolized the table, mesmerizing the group with his riveting stories.

We all walked out to the parking lot together. Levy looked at me with a devious smirk. The man was interesting to listen to, but he could not be trusted as far as one could spit.

Tom and I were discussing the benefits of fresh spring water when Lester came over and interrupted. "Grant, how do you know so much? Nobody else tonight could follow what I was saying. You are quite unusual."

I replied, "You did most of the talking, I just listened. I'm a good listener."

Lester looked at me and laughed, as if to say *I wasn't born yesterday*. I laughed along with him.

I asked him how long he had known Levy.

"Levy? Oh, a few years. I fill up my water containers at his house every week because he has a wonderful water filtration system." Lester gave me an appraising look and said, "You know, I think you would like working with us. In another division, of course, due to your particular background."

I was taken aback. Work with whom? I replied, "Well, thank you, I'll think about it."

We shook hands, then Lester said good night to everyone and left.

I laughed to myself. The last thing I wanted to be called was *the one that got recruited*.

Levy was still in the lot, talking to another guy from the group. I walked over to Levy and said, "Your friend is an interesting person."

He smiled. "Oh yes, that's for sure."

I said, "*Is* he your friend?"

"Well, yes, sort of."

"Sort of? What do you mean, sort of? Isn't he your guest tonight? Didn't you bring him to the group?"

"Yes. So?"

"Well, how well do you know him?" I asked.

"I know him for about four months, but I'm not that close a friend."

"So, you hardly know him?"

He shrugged. "I suppose."

I said, "Why would you bring someone you hardly know to our dinner table?"

He replied, "He seems nice enough." Then he turned away, saying, "I've got to go." He was laughing to himself, his eyes shifty.

He jumped into his car and took off like a bat out of hell.

Lester had said they'd known one another a few years, Levy said a few months. One of them had lied, right to my face.

What did Levy have to hide? The pieces were beginning to fit together. The more I thought about it, the more it made sense. My gut instinct was that Levy too was a government agent or some kind of agent.

I asked Tom who had invited Levy and he said he had.

"How long have you known Levy?" I asked.

Tom said, "I just met him a few weeks ago, at a convention."

"So you really don't know him from beans?"

Tom replied, "That's right, Grant."

"How well do you know Lester?"

"I just met Lester last week when Levy brought him as a guest."

"So these people are pretty much strangers."

Tom replied, "I suppose so."

I said, "Tom, how long have you known the rest of the group at our table?"

"Oh, I know all of them for many years…" He looked at me and asked, "Is something wrong?"

I replied, "No, everything is fine."

Tom didn't know about the problems I'd had in the past with this type of character. It seemed that they had infiltrated Tom's little group, for whatever reason.

And Tom's group was a Christian bible group. This proved to me there were no limits when it came to gathering information and keeping tabs on persons of interest.

From that point on, when Tom would call me to remind me of the weekly get-together at the local diner, I would ignore him. I saw red flags everywhere and avoided his calls. I couldn't call Tom back, or else I would have had to explain things I didn't want to talk about. So I just didn't call him or show up. It was tense to say the least.

CHAPTER 21

NEIGHBORS

The next day, in my never-ending search for good health and improved well-being, I stumbled on a new product. A friend of mine had told me about this amazing new device, claiming it had the ability to bring peace and harmony to any area it was activated in. My friend Rod said he had purchased this strange device from a friend who taught yoga.

He showed it to me. It looked like nothing special, just a little box the size of a deck of cards.

Rod said, "I only used this device a few times, but it was very pleasant. You're welcome to try it out for a few days. Maybe it will help you become more relaxed so you can focus better on your projects."

I asked, "So how does this device make you feel?"

He smiled beatifically. "I feel very relaxed whenever I use it. It seems to do what it's supposed to do. Do you want to borrow it for a few days? I know how you like to investigate new things."

Why not?

I said, "Sure, I'll give it a shot, see what it does and how it makes me feel."

Rod handed me the little box and I put it in my jacket pocket.

When I got home, I cooked lamb chops accompanied by pure mint jelly and a baked potato with a dollop of sour cream. I sipped some Merlot from a vineyard on the north fork of Long Island. My friend and his family ran the James Port Vineyard, and they produced some of the finest Merlot in the Northeast. They had won several awards for their wine.

As I sat in the living room after dinner, I remembered the device Rod had loaned me. I took the box out of my jacket pocket, switched it on, and placed it on a table near where I was sitting. Then I waited for something to happen.

A few minutes went by, but I didn't feel any changes in the room or in my body. I decided to turn on a movie, a romantic comedy. I had seemed to gravitate toward the lighter movies of late, rather than the thrillers and mysteries, the dark dramas I used to like. Maybe I was becoming a romantic.

As the movie started, I relaxed a bit. My neck had been bothering me earlier, but it didn't hurt so much anymore. Not as much as it had earlier in the day. I wondered if the device was working or if it was just my imagination.

As the movie continued, I realized I wasn't obsessing like I normally did. In fact, my mind was a calm cool blank. As the movie progressed, so did the feeling of relaxation and a sense of peace. I felt loose. My neck didn't hurt at all.

I thought to myself, oh my god, this thing of Rod's actually works!

I watched the rest of the movie and enjoyed it more than I had when I saw it in the theatre. I was smiling ear to ear, experiencing a wonderful sense of tranquility. That certainly wasn't a product of my imagination.

After the movie ended, I turned off the device and made myself Belgian hot cocoa with organic whipped cream. This was a ritual I performed every night now before retiring for the evening.

I sat down with my cocoa to watch the late night talk show with my old friend from the private party I'd crashed in New York, back before he was famous. I smiled. Jimmy was interviewing a sexy celebrity I had a crush on.

As I sat there watching my show and sipping my hot cocoa, the whipped cream melting into the warm chocolate, I realized I was enjoying my late night ritual more than I usually did. In fact, I was grinning like an idiot. I figured this was a residual effect from using the device. Leftover bliss combined with some of the finest hot cocoa and the best whipped cream available. The combination was absolutely spectacular.

CYNTHIA

That night, I slept soundly. I woke up feeling refreshed, ready for breakfast and hot coffee. I got up and made myself some scrambled eggs with toast and jelly. I also prepared a pot of my favorite coffee after blending the beans and grinding them, another ritual.

My brewing coffee smelled so good that my neighbor knocked on my door. Cynthia said, "Hey Grant, I can smell that coffee from a block away! It smells divine! Can I try some?"

"Of course, come on in," I replied. "Please sit down and make yourself at home. Do you take cream and sugar?"

Cynthia nodded. "Yes, please. Regular sugar, extra cream."

I said, "That's exactly how I prefer my coffee." We smiled at one another.

Cynthia said, "Some of the neighbors have been commenting on how wonderful your coffee always smells. If you keep it up, you'll soon have a line at your door!"

We both laughed.

I replied, "Well, I must be doing something right, then. So, do you want to know what my secret is?"

"Yes!" She sat forward in her chair at the kitchen table.

I said "Okay, if you promise not to tell anyone, I will share my secret recipe for extra delicious coffee."

She nodded, leaned toward me, her eyes sparkling. She was quite pretty in the morning light.

I said, "I take some of my favorite coffee beans from different parts of the world and grind them together. The end product is nothing less than exquisite. I can't start my day any other way."

We both burst out laughing.

When we calmed down, I said, "I'm serious, Cynthia, this is what I have grown accustomed to. When I go out for coffee, it doesn't seem like anyone can get it right. It never tastes the way I like my coffee to taste."

She said, "Grant, that's because nobody makes coffee the way you do. It would cost them a fortune!"

"I know," I said with a quick laugh. "And that's why you always see me with a Thermos."

I handed Cynthia her coffee. "I hope I made it the way you like it. I prepared it the way I make my own coffee."

Cynthia took a sip, smiled, and said, "Oh my god, Grant, I've never had coffee like this! It's like heaven in my mouth!"

I quipped, "I know what else would be like heaven in your mouth."

Cynthia grinned. "Oh Grant, don't tempt me. Anybody that can make coffee like this is worth taking a closer look at."

She sipped her coffee, eyeing me carefully. Then she said, "I was a barista for years, working at a café to help put myself through school. We never made coffee taste the way you do."

I smiled. "And that's not all I'm good at."

I was really flirting heavily. Fortunately, Cynthia had a sense of humor. She laughed. Then she said, "I have to go before I get myself in trouble. Besides, I don't want to be late for work."

I said, "I'll be around later, if you want to drop by again," and smiled at her.

As I opened the door to let Cynthia out, our smiles lingered. She winked at me, then walked away. I closed the door.

PABLO

I sat down in the living room. My friend's device was staring me in the face. I was curious about how it worked and I debated about whether to unscrew the back and open up the unit. I thought if I didn't open it, I'd never have an idea how it did what it did.

So, I did the unthinkable. I grabbed my screwdriver, undid the screws, and opened up the device.

Inside was an antenna coil made of copper wrapped many times in a tight little circle. There was a battery, a circuit board, all the expected parts. None that were out of the ordinary. The antenna struck me as strange, and elaborate, but the weirdest item in the device was neatly tucked and wrapped around the coil: a small piece of paper.

Now, I had seen all types of things in my days. But paper? I wasn't an engineer, so most of the time I really didn't know what I was looking at when I took something apart. But paper?

I didn't want to touch the circuitry, but now I was even more curious about how it worked. One of my neighbors was an electrical engineer. Pablo was real smart. A quiet man, he was married to a nice woman named Patty.

I knocked on Pablo's door. He answered. "Grant, how are you? Is there something I can help you with?"

I said, "Yes, actually. My friend loaned me an electrical device that helps you relax by creating a harmonious environment. I was wondering if you would take a gander at this thing and let me know what you think of it."

Pablo said, "Sure that sounds interesting. I'm always open to looking at things when I have the time. I'm off today. Your timing is good. Come on in."

I stepped inside Pablo's condo. The place was bigger than mine, and it was nice and clean. I followed him into the kitchen and we sat across from one another at a round oak table. Pablo said, "Would you like a beer?"

I said, "No thanks, but a glass of cold water would be good."

He replied, "Sure, you're in luck. I just finished installing my new water purifier unit. It takes everything out that's bad, and leaves you with pure water."

"Sounds great!"

Pablo handed me a glass of cold water. I took a sip. The water tasted clean and crisp.

Pablo said, "Okay, bro, let's see what you have there."

I took the device out of my pocket and put it on the table next to my water glass. Pablo picked it up. He unscrewed the back, and took a good look inside.

I asked, "So what do you see?"

Pablo replied, "I need to use a stronger light source."

He left the room. He came back wearing a miner's headband with a strong light attached to it, similar to what a doctor would wear during surgery.

Pablo studied the device for a few minutes. Then he said, "Okay, I know what this is, and I know what this is, but what the hell is *this*?" He pointed to the paper.

I replied, "I don't know. That's why I came to you, Pablo."

We both laughed.

Pablo hooked it up to an oscilloscope to perform a function analysis test and see what it produced. He said, "This thing is really interesting. This may sound strange, but I can feel it working on me. I think I want one for myself. It seems like a very simple design. After looking at it like this, I think I can probably build my own."

I replied, "Probably, but you still haven't answered my question. How does it work? Like what's *that* for?" I pointed to the coil.

"That is a very strange geometrical antenna coil, one that I never encountered before. As for the paper, I can't tell you. I have no idea what it's for."

I said, "Could it be there to prevent the antenna from touching the circuitry?"

Pablo replied, "No, that's not it. Do you want me to slide it out of there so we can see what it is?"

"Can you do that without damaging it?"

"Sure. I can take this whole thing apart and put it back together with my eyes closed now, I've studied it long enough. Plus, it's simple."

Simple for him, maybe. I said, "Okay, but be very careful because it's not mine."

Pablo gingerly removed the paper from around the coil. He said, "Wow, look! It's a scroll!"

I started to lean forward. "Let me see it."

I held out my hand. A scroll?

I unrolled it carefully. There was a lot of tiny text on it. The print was strange, more like hieroglyphics than letters. Neither of us could figure out what it meant.

I asked him, "Can you make a copy of it so I can show some people who might know how to decipher this?"

Pablo replied, "Sure, I have a printer in my office."

He printed a copy and handed it to me, then tucked the scroll back in place around the coil and closed up the unit.

We both sat back in our chairs and looked at one another. Finally, Pablo smiled and said, "Bro that is some weird stuff! I'm glad you're my neighbor. Who else would knock on my door and ask me to help solve a mystery?"

I replied, "Isn't that what neighbors are for?"

We both laughed.

Pablo said, "Are you sure I can't offer you a beer?"

"Maybe next time. I should go. I have to get to the bottom of this mystery."

Pablo nodded. "So you'll keep me posted, right?"

I told him I would.

CHAPTER 22

THE SCROLL

That night, I tried looking on the Internet for information on scrolls. There were plenty of articles, but nothing related to what I needed to know. It seemed everything I found online was a dead end.

I went to bed early and found myself twisting and turning. I kept thinking about the scroll and what it might mean. Who could I get to decipher it for me?

Then I thought of my old friend Nikko. When I had worked at Nordstrom in the fine jewelry department, the manager and I became good friends. We sold jewelry together. Whenever somebody with any type of accent walked in looking for a piece of jewelry, my manager would speak to them in their language. No matter what language they spoke. So if I encountered a customer from a foreign country, I would immediately turn them over to Nikko because I knew he could speak their native tongue. Then we would split the commission. This worked out well for me.

Nikko had told me that when he lived in Greece he had worked as an interpreter for the Army. Nikko was a polyglot, and he spoke something like seventeen languages. To me, that was absolutely amazing. I was still working on my English skills.

Nikko had given me his phone number years ago. I wondered if I could find it. I stored all my telephone numbers and business cards in a plastic bag.

I jumped out of bed and began to search frantically for the bag. If anyone would know what the scroll said, it would be Nikko.

When I unearthed the bag in a bureau drawer, I was thrilled. That bag contained almost every business card and phone number I had ever received. I had a lot of work ahead of me. There were thousands of numbers for me to go through.

I sat back on the bed and started looking at the numbers, examining them one by one.

As the hours went by, I grew tired. I told myself that was it, one more handful and I was going back to bed.

That's not it, that's not it, not it, not it...

I found it! I yelled out loud. *Whoopee!*

I fell back on my bed and stretched out with a big smile. But the joy quickly faded. It had been years since Nikko had given me his number. Maybe nine, almost ten years. Would he still have the same phone number?

That would be a miracle, I thought before I dozed off.

The next day I made myself some of my famous coffee. The coffee that had the whole neighborhood buzzing. Then I telephoned Nikko to see if the number was still in service.

It was ringing, and ringing, and ringing. I waited for the voicemail of a stranger to click on.

"Hello?"

I said in surprise, "Hello!"

He said, "Who's this?"

I asked the same.

He said, "But you dialed me, and your number's private."

I said, "You're right. This is Grant."

I could hear raucous laughter on the other end of the phone. "Grant, you dropped off the planet, I never heard from you. I heard you'd moved to Florida," he managed to say when he was done laughing.

I said, "Nikko, is it really you?"

He laughed and said, "Who were you expecting?"

I replied, "I don't know. People change their numbers, they get cell phones, they lose their phones. Numbers change all the time."

Nikko said, "Not mine, my friend. Too many people need to reach me."

I said with deep joy, "Nikko, how have you been?"

He replied, "Good, very good, everything is fine. How are you, Grant? Are you still in Florida?"

"Yes, and it's beautiful here. It must be freezing up in New York."

He laughed and said, "My friend, I'm in Florida too."

"You're in Florida? Who let *you* in?"

We laughed.

He said, "Grant, you're still the same."

I said, "Who were you expecting?" and we laughed some more. I asked, "Whereabouts in Florida are you?"

"I'm in Palm Beach."

"Really? Wow, I can't believe it, you're right nearby! I'm just south of you. How long have you lived here?"

"Sandy and I have been here for seven months."

I didn't know his wife but I remembered her name was Sandy. I replied, "That's so great! How do you like it?"

"We love it. No more snow or cold weather, just lots of sun. So what made you decide to call me after all this time?"

"I thought of you yesterday because I need to talk to someone who knows languages. I discovered this scroll and the text is written in a language I don't recognize. I thought if anyone could interpret it, it would be you, Nikko."

"So you tracked me down, and now you want me to take a look at this scroll to let you know what it says?"

"Yes."

"Grant, you're a lucky bastard. You're lucky that you found my number, that my number still works and, most of all, that I live just north of you. Of course I'll help you. What could be simpler?"

I replied, "I guess it was meant to be."

Nikko said, "We can meet tomorrow for lunch and I'll take a look at this scroll for you. Where did you get it?"

"It's a long story. I'll tell you when I see you."

"Call me in the morning and we'll figure out where to meet."

I was a lucky guy, all right.

The next morning I called Nikko and we set up a place and time to meet.

When I arrived at the diner, Nikko was seated in a booth. He looked the same except he was tan. We shook hands, laughed, ordered food, and talked about old times.

Over coffee, Nikko said, "So let's see the scroll." He called the waitress over to clean off our table. After she left, I took the tiny copy of the scroll out of my pocket and handed it to him.

Nikko began to laugh. "*That's* your scroll? I was expecting to see something a lot larger than this!"

I said, "It's what's written on the scroll that's important. Right?"

He nodded. "Of course you're right, Grant."

He took out his reading glasses and studied the tiny text. "Yes, I need these to read now. I didn't need them when you knew me ten years ago."

I said, "That's fine, we all get older. But in your case I don't know what to think."

He laughed, and then said, "Do you want me to read the scroll?"

"Yes, I'll be quiet."

Nikko was silent, his focus intense. After about fifteen minutes, he took off his glasses and looked at me. "Grant, where did you get this?"

"I discovered it inside a device my friend loaned me."

"What kind of device?"

After I described the device in detail, Nikko said, "I never heard of a device like that. Surely your friend did not buy this in a normal department store?"

I shook my head.

"So where did he get it?"

"He bought it from a friend who teaches yoga and meditation."

Nikko replied, "Okay, I see. That makes sense because the text is ancient Sanskrit."

Sanskrit?

He pointed to the tiny symbols and said, "These are not sentences, they're words that represent things. They're symbols. But symbols are like jigsaw puzzles, you have to piece them together to know what they mean. For example, this symbol means ocean, and this symbol means sky, and this one means land. There must be over fifty of these symbols, but we will never know what it means unless you find someone who actually knows *all* the symbols."

"Is it like Hebrew?"

"To a degree, yes. It's two languages combined together."

I asked him if he thought I could bring the scroll to a rabbi. He said it was unlikely a rabbi could help.

"Do you know *anyone* I can show this to?" I asked.

"No," Nikko replied. Then he told me he was sorry he couldn't help.

After lunch, I said, "It was nice catching up, so don't be a stranger now that we live so close."

Nikko replied, "You don't be a stranger either, my friend."

We hugged and parted ways.

THE RABBI

The next morning, I woke up early. After breakfast, I went on the computer and looked up the local synagogues. I would try a rabbi; see if one might be able to help me. I would find a conservative temple, one with a rabbi who adhered to strict rules and followed the old traditions to the letter. A rabbi like that might have some insight into what was printed on the scroll.

I located an orthodox temple and drove over. I parked in the parking lot and walked to the front door. The temple also had a Hebrew school. A woman standing in the entrance introduced herself and told me she was the school principal.

Helene was friendly and asked if she could help me with something. I showed her the copy of the scroll and asked her if she could read it. She said she would give it a shot and took a close look at it.

She studied it for a minute, and then said, "That's interesting. It doesn't have any sentences, just symbols."

I said, "A friend of mine told me the same thing. That's why I'm here. I wondered if the rabbi might understand the symbols."

She said, "Wait here just a moment."

I asked, "Where are you going?"

She replied, "The rabbi has a class once a month with all the children. It looks like the class is letting out. Maybe I can have the rabbi take a look at this for you to see what he says. Now *I* need to know what it means too," she said with a smile.

I waited just inside the doorway. After a while, the rabbi came over to greet me. He shook my hand and gave me a warm smile. He seemed very nice. He said, "Hello, I'm Rabbi Gold."

I introduced myself and said, "I'm sorry to bother you, I know you're very busy."

The rabbi replied, "No bother, happy to help."

He had the scroll in his hand, so he gave it back to me. He said, "I understand what the words mean, but none of it makes sense. It's in ancient Sanskrit. My guess is it has something to do with Jewish mysticism. That's as much as I can tell you, if that helps you at all."

Jewish mysticism? How cool!

I replied, "That helps me a great deal, Rabbi Gold. Now I have a direction to search in. Up until now, it's been a wild goose chase."

The rabbi laughed.

I thanked him and he said, "You are very welcome. And you are welcome to come to the temple anytime."

After he walked away, Helene came over and said, "Did you find out what it means? Was the rabbi able to help you?"

I replied, "Yes and no. I mean, now I know where to look. The scroll is written in Vedic Sanskrit. The rabbi was not able to decipher the meaning, though."

Helene said, "This is just like something from the movies!"

I said, "I know! Now I have to find someone who can decipher Vedic Sanskrit."

Helene said, "Why don't you try the Kabbalah Center in Boca?"

I'd had no idea there was such a place. And right nearby.

Helene said, "I'll write down the address and telephone number for you. But only on one condition."

I asked, "What condition is that?"

"When you find out what the symbols mean, you must promise to stop by here or call me and let me know."

"Definitely. It's a deal."

Helene wrote down all the information about the Kabbalah Center on the back of her business card and handed it to me. I thanked her and said, "I've got to run over there right now, it's getting late. They probably close at five."

As I was walking out the door, she called after me. "Grant, Grant!"

I turned around. "Yes, Helene?"

"I meant to ask you, where did you find that scroll."

I smiled and said, "That's a whole other story. Let's save that for another time."

Helene smiled and gave me a cute wave goodbye.

CHAPTER 23

THE KABBALAH CENTER

I drove south to the Kabbalah Center. I parked my car in the packed lot and walked over to the visitors' entrance. The building had high ceilings and an impressive modern décor. I stood in the vestibule admiring the minimalist architecture.

A tall gentleman accompanied by a young, dark haired woman appeared in the lobby and welcomed me to the Kabbalah Center. The man asked, "How can we help you?"

I replied, "Does anyone here read Hebrew and Sanskrit?"

The gentleman said, "Why do you ask?"

"My name is Grant. And you are?"

He smiled. "I'm Marc, and this is my assistant Susan."

"It's a pleasure to meet both of you," I said with a smile. "The reason I'm here is I have in my possession an old scroll. I need the text on it translated. I don't know what it says or what it means or even what it's for. I'm hoping someone here might be able to help me with this."

Marc nodded. "Wait here. Just one moment."

Susan excused herself to do some paperwork and Marc went into a back office. He came out with an old fellow with a long salt-and-pepper beard.

"Hello, my name is David," the elderly man said. We shook hands, and David said, "Marc says you have a scroll of some sort?"

I replied, "Yes, I was hoping you could help me out with this wild goose chase I've been on."

David smiled, then said, "May I offer you something to drink?"

"Yes, please. Do you have any cold water? It's so hot out today."

"Why don't you sit down and relax at the table over there and we'll get you a cold drink."

I sat down with David while Marc went to get my drink from the back room. He returned with a bottle of spring water and a glass filled with ice. I thanked him and drank it down quickly.

David said, "You must have been really thirsty."

I laughed and agreed that I was.

David asked, "Do you have the scroll with you?"

I took out the copy of the scroll and handed it to David. He studied it, and then handed it to Marc.

David looked across the table at me. "Grant, where did you find this?"

"I'll tell you the whole story, but first please tell me what the text means. Do you know what the scroll is for?"

David said, "The text on the scroll appears to be the equations that can provide the answer to a very difficult and complex cryptogram. Once deciphered, the information on this scroll may hold the key to unlocking the passages and doorways through the barriers mankind have longed to experience in this universe for centuries."

What? I held still, not speaking, barely breathing.

He continued, never taking his eyes from mine, "Therefore, the person who possesses these equations, once decoded and carefully modified into symbology, will experience a wonderful transformation, a radical paradigm shift. This scroll is the prerequisite for the journey of transcendence. That is, transcending beyond what we humans know as reality to where a fabulous new world emerges. The realm of being where love, compassion, and happiness exist for all and for all time."

I sat back in my chair. It took me a few minutes to process what David had just said. It seemed like an awful lot to absorb and understand. Marc was still studying the text on the copy of the scroll.

Finally, I said, "David, what you just said is absolutely mindboggling. So, is the scroll sacred? Is it ancient? Is it meant to be kept hidden from us, from all modern day humans?"

David replied, "Yes, it is most likely sacred, very old, and a secret. It's quite amazing, isn't it?" When I nodded, he stiffened, suddenly concerned. "You haven't told people about this, have you?"

"No, not really."

David relaxed. "Good. I would suggest you keep it that way."

I said okay.

David stared at me, his dark eyes intense. "Now tell me, how did you come upon this scroll? You do have the original, correct?" When I nodded, he said, "It's not every day a sacred scroll the ancient mystics once used just falls out of the sky and lands in a young man's lap."

I laughed. True, but it had happened to me.

I said, "David, I must admit I wasn't exploring the catacombs of Egypt when I found the scroll."

David replied, "So if you didn't dig it up somewhere, where did you find it?"

Marc looked up from the scroll, his eyes on me. They both waited for my explanation.

Before I could speak, David held up a hand to stall me, then called out, "Susan, if anyone calls for Marc or myself, tell them we're at a meeting and will call back when we're finished."

Susan replied from her desk across the room, "Okay, no problem."

"Grant, you now have our undivided attention. So tell us how you came into possession of this artifact."

I told them about my friend Rod and his offer to lend me the relaxation device he had received from his friend the yoga instructor. I told them how the device had worked to relax me and help heal up my neck pain. "Even after I turned off the device, the feeling of peacefulness lingered throughout the rest of the evening."

David said, "That sounds like a profound experience."

"It was," I replied.

He nodded. "And what does the scroll have to do with all this?"

I explained how I had taken apart the device to find out how it worked. "Wrapped around a coil inside was a piece of paper. A scroll."

Marc and David looked at one another, brows raised.

I went on with my story about how I had consulted Pablo, the Orthodox rabbi, and the suggestion that had led me to them. I said, "Wouldn't an Orthodox rabbi know what the text meant?"

David replied, "No, only a rabbi who had studied Jewish mysticism."

Marc said, "Fascinating story."

David smiled and said, "I agree." He looked at me, running his stubby fingers through his beard. "Now, wouldn't it be interesting to find out who the builder of the device is? Because whoever built it had the scroll. And whoever had possession of the scroll possesses great knowledge. Ancient knowledge of the mystical kind."

I got excited. "Of course! I need to find the inventor of the device. The builder will be able to tell me exactly what the scroll says."

CHAPTER 24

RETRO

Back at the condo, I ate dinner and tried to calm myself. This was so exciting! Mystical information, an ancient scroll in Vedic Sanskrit text, a radical paradigm shift transcending beyond reality into the realm of love, compassion, and happiness? Wow. Who could have imagined that I, Grant Davis, would stumble on the key to this ancient wisdom?

That evening, I set out on the next phase of my journey. My new mission was to find the man behind the machine. The inventor of the device, the builder.

I needed to speak with Rod and find out about the yoga instructor. But I was on my way to South Beach to visit my friend Len. I dialed Rod's number, and the call went right to voicemail.

I left a message. "Rod, call me when you get this message, it's very important!"

Driving south to Miami, the highway was clear. The sun was setting, and in the darkening sky was the largest full moon I had ever seen. It was something else, so full and blindingly bright. A super moon. But I had to keep my eyes in the road, because driving in Miami was always crazy. And with a full moon like that, all the loonies would be out. Many of them would be behind the wheel.

I wasn't far from the turnoff to South Beach when it started to rain. I turned on my wipers and drove more slowly. I was beginning to lose visibility. The rain came down so hard I could barely see. It started to thunder, and then the lightning kicked in. Finally I was forced to put on my hazard lights and pull into the far right lane.

I exited the highway and headed east to the ocean. Then I drove down a side street and parked my car. I tried to call Len but I had no signal on my cell phone.

The lightning and thunder were incessant. The wind was strong, gusting around the car. These types of sudden, violent storms had always made me nervous. "Right Here, Right Now" was on the radio. I sang the lyrics, trying to calm myself.

There I was, by myself, trapped in my car with no cell phone signal, stuck. Then my gas light went on. The tank was on empty.

Great, I said to myself sarcastically as I turned off the engine. Just great.

What I needed to do was relax and wait for the storm to blow over. In Florida, these storms usually didn't last long. They came and went with a vengeance, though. And it was an electrical storm, the most dangerous kind.

I remembered I had the device with me somewhere in my duffel bag. I reached behind the seat for my bag and went through it frantically, looking for the device.

There it was in a zippered pocket. I tossed the bag on the passenger seat and pressed the switch that turned on the device. Then I leaned back against the headrest and closed my eyes. The song still played in my head. *Right here, right now...*

Oh my, there was that feeling again, that sense of well-being and calmness. Just what I needed. I sighed with pleasure. I was going to feel better in a few minutes. *Right here, right now...*

Something strange began to happen. My body was moving. It felt as if the car was being shaken. The vibration increased until my head was throbbing. What the hell was happening?

I looked out the window and saw nothing but dark sky and pouring rain. Nobody was out there messing with my car. Nobody was around.

The car shook violently and the storm raged around me. *Right here, right now...*

Suddenly there was a loud blast; as if it were the Fourth of July and someone had lit an M-80 firecracker right beside the car. *Boom!*

I closed my eyes again and clutched the device, hoping the chaos would end soon. The car gradually stopped shaking and my heart stopped racing.

When I opened my eyes, it was sunny and beautiful. The rain had stopped. I looked more closely at the sun-dappled streets. It was as if it had never rained at all. No puddles, no drifting storm clouds, no fronds shaken loose in the wild wind.

No super moon. And the sun was high in the sky. Huh?

I turned off the device and put it back in my duffel bag. I opened the car door, stepped out and looked around. The sun was bright, the birds sang. I couldn't spot a puddle anywhere. It was more than strange, to say the least.

I slapped myself to see if I'd wake up because I thought I must be dreaming. I figured if I slapped myself hard enough, I would come to my senses. I had left my place at dusk, driven a couple dozen miles, stopped for a violent storm, and now it was morning? A sunny gorgeous morning?

At this point, I was very confused. As I walked by the Fontainebleau, a landmark hotel on Miami Beach, a woman yelled, "Hey! Why are you slapping yourself?"

I looked behind me and across the street, but I couldn't find her.

She yelled, "Up here, I'm up here!"

A pretty young woman with blonde hair waved from one of the hotel balconies. The hotel itself looked strange, not as modern as I remembered. How odd.

I yelled up to her, "Hi there, I'm Grant."

She replied, "I'm Jennifer."

"Nice to meet you, Jennifer."

"It's nice to meet you too. But you didn't answer my question. Why were you slapping yourself?"

I thought about it. "Jennifer, it's so beautiful today and I can't believe I'm here, in Miami."

"Well, you certainly are! I can see you, and I'm talking to you, right?"

"Yes, but everything looks so different."

She frowned. "Different from what?"

I said, "Do you want to come down and talk with me? I'm tired of yelling. I need to sit down and have something cold to drink. I could really use some company."

She paused to consider. Then she said, "Okay, you seem nice enough. Maybe a little confused, but nice. I'll be right down. Meet me in the lobby lounge."

JENNY JENNY

I went inside and found the lounge. The theme was retro. Zebra stripes, disco balls. There was a patio outside so I selected a table in the sun.

When Jennifer arrived, I stood up to greet her. The girl had had some figure! Could I have been any luckier?

She was dressed in a retro style. She wore a short tight dress, the kind all the women wore back in the 1980s. The dress had puffy shoulders, and it was neon pink. She also wore a matching set of dangling earrings. Chunky heels. I thought her outfit was odd, but she could get away with it because she was so gorgeous.

Jennifer smiled as she sat down with me at the little white table. I was gawking at her. She laughed and stared back at me.

Finally Jennifer said, "Grant, you dress weird, but I like it."

Me? I laughed. "I was just thinking the same thing about you."

She frowned. "You think *I'm* dressed weird? What do you want, it's 1981. The seventies are over, man!"

I smiled. She was strange but very appealing.

A gray haired waiter came over to take our order, so I ordered us a round of drinks.

After he left, Jennifer said, "Like, where did you get those clothes, Grant?"

I looked around at the people in the lounge, in the lobby, on the beach. Everyone was dressed like it was decades in the past. Men had styled hair; women wore their hair equally short and blown dry. The colors were pastel, the outfits patterned and with wide shoulders. It was weird. It felt like I'd wandered into an event, 1980s Day at the Fontainebleau.

Was this a costume party I had stumbled on?

Jennifer said, "Where are you from?"

I replied, "New York."

She said, "Even in New York City, they don't dress like you!" Then she laughed.

I felt like a freak. My outfit would not work if I wanted to spend time with this hot woman at the hip Fontainebleau. And I did. What guy wouldn't?

Thinking fast, I said, "Do you know of a local thrift shop where I can get some clothes?"

She replied, "Are you incognito, Grant? Hiding from someone?"

"Maybe," I winked and flashed her mysterious little smile.

"There's obviously a story that goes with this, right, Grant? So if I help you, do you promise to tell me?"

I said, "Yes, I promise. So come on, let's get out of here."

We walked down the block and Jennifer led me into a small shop. The racks were lined with some of the most creative, chic, designer clothing from the early eighties. Totally retro but new looking. Wow.

With Jennifer's help, I found some jeans that fit and a few nice shirts, along with a bathing suit. The prices weren't cheap, though, considering the fashions had gone out of style decades before.

I paid for everything in cash and changed into my new clothes in the dressing room. Then I had the manager bag up the rest, along with my own clothes. As I was walking out, the manager asked, "How much you want for the clothes you were wearing when you came in here?"

I said, "Really?"

He nodded. He gave me an odd look. "I like the outfit, very unusual. How much you want for it?"

I thought about it. Unusual? Everybody dressed in Cuban shirts and linen slacks like mine. But money was money, no matter how strange my life had suddenly become.

I said, "Give me half my cash back and the newspaper you're reading and we'll call it even."

He nodded, so I took my old clothes out of one of the shopping bags. As I handed them over, he said, "Where're you from?"

I said, "New York, but sometimes I feel like I'm from another planet."

He looked up from pawing through my clothes and said, "You'd have to be to wear these things!"

We all laughed.

Jennifer and I left the thrift shop and kept walking south. We stopped to pick up a few slices of pizza, some potato chips, a couple cans of juice. Boy was the food cheap here in this part of Miami Beach.

We headed for the sand. It was a beautiful day and the beach was packed with sun worshippers. The fragrance of tropical tanning oil filled the air. We found a bench to sit on so we could relax, eat, and talk.

While Jennifer got the food out of the brown bags, I glanced at the newspaper. The date at the top was May 19, 1981.

Was the whole city in on this joke? Was it retro day in all of Miami?

I looked at Jennifer. She gave me that look. The kind when the person doesn't say a word, they just lift their eyebrows and allow a little smile to peek through.

I said, "I promised you I would tell you everything, but first let's eat our pizza before it gets cold."

We smiled at one another, and then dug in.

After a couple minutes, she said with her mouth full of pizza, "You better tell me everything!"

I laughed and said, "I will."

"Somehow, I don't believe you."

"I always keep my word."

"Okay, I'm going to hold you to that."

I said, "Don't hold me too tight, I still need to breathe."

We both laughed, and then she threw some potato chips at me.

After we finished eating, Jennifer said, "I'm ready, so tell me, tell me!"

I replied, "Look, Jennifer, you might think I'm making this up, but I'm going to tell you the honest to god truth. Okay? I mean, even if you don't believe me, remember this: my clothes don't lie. Okay?"

She nodded, her expression puzzled. "Go on."

"Last night I was driving to Miami to visit a friend of mine named Len."

Jennifer asked, "Where were you coming from?"

"I had just come from speaking to some Jewish mystics."

"Jewish mystics?"

"Yes, I was in Boca and I went to a center where Jewish mysticism is taught and practiced."

Jennifer replied, "Wow! That's different."

She thought that was different? Wait until she heard the rest.

I said, "Well, I found this ancient scroll, and I needed to know more about it. I didn't know where to start, until I met up with a friend of mine..."

Her face went from confused to interested to disbelieving to confused again as I told her the story about the scroll and the people I had discussed it with, ending with the visit to the Kabbalah Center.

"So what did the Jewish mystics say?" Jennifer asked.

I hesitated. I couldn't tell her that. David had told me to keep mum, and he was right, that would be best for now. So I shook my head. "I can't tell you just yet."

"Why?" Jennifer sipped her juice.

"Because I love teasing you, and I'm having too much of a good time doing it."

"Grant, I'm going to kick your butt if you don't!"

I smiled. She was fun, I enjoyed her company. And she was so nice to look at, with those long tanned limbs and that big white smile.

"Let's wait until later," I said with a grin.

"No! Please, please, tell me. I'll do anything!"

"Anything?"

"Yes, anything!"

"Okayyyyy. Well, the men at the center told me it was nothing."

"I don't believe that for one minute. Liar!"

She *had* said anything, right? I sighed. "Okay, they said the text is the key, if you will, to unlock and release all things that are wonderful in this universe, to make the world the most magnificent and beautiful place to ever exist."

Jennifer laughed. "Sure. Grant that sounds like something out of a fairytale!"

"I know! But that's what they said. And now I need to find the builder, the person who invented this device and embedded the scroll."

She pushed me, and then punched me lightly on the shoulder. She thought I was joking around.

"I'm dead serious," I told her.

She frowned. "Grant, I am going to have to kick your ass!"

Then she jumped on top of me and got me in a headlock.

After we wrangled for a minute, I said, "Okay, okay! Just don't hurt me!"

Jennifer let go, but she stayed close in case she needed to apply another headlock.

I said, "Look, somewhere out there is the person who built a device based on a scroll from the ancient mystics, a scroll that can release the energies of good throughout the universe. And when you use the device containing that scroll, you feel awesome. Peaceful, totally well. But last night when I used it during a thunderstorm, something weird happened. And now, here I am. It's confusing."

She gave me the look again, so I told her what happened after I parked near the hotel during the storm.

Jennifer said, "But it didn't rain last night."

"It was raining where I was last night, and it was a hot evening. The moon was huge, fuller than full. It was 2014! I used the device and now here I am with you on a sunny day in May, 1981." I sighed. "I have to admit, though, I really loved the eighties."

Jennifer didn't laugh and say, *don't be silly, Grant, it isn't 1981.* She was staring at me with a strange look on her face. "Are you sure nobody slipped you something? Some acid or something?"

"No, that isn't what happened. It's something else, and it has to do with the scroll and the device," I replied.

"Okay, well, you said there was a big fat moon, right? So did you know the full moon opens up portals and vortexes? I mean, everybody knows that."

I replied, "So how come nobody told me? How do you know all this, Jennifer?"

"My mom has been an astrologer for over twenty years. She told me about all the different phases of the moon, and the effects they have on the earth."

"So what are portals?"

Jennifer explained patiently, "Portals are energy centers on the earth that open up and dilate again whenever the moon is full. When this occurs, there's no predicting what can happen!" She thought for a moment. Then she exclaimed, "Grant, you were here in Miami Beach!"

I replied, "So? What does that have to do with anything?"

She leaned forward and said, "My dad is a meteorologist and a professional diver. He explores sunken ships. He told me recently that a good portion of Miami Beach is in the Bermuda triangle."

Right. I knew that.

Jennifer said, "See, most of it is in the ocean, but there are three points on a triangle. One of these points reaches into Miami Beach, into the bay area."

I replied, "I've read about that, yes."

"So you must know that the Bermuda triangle is considered a major vortex. And, see, you were in it during the storm! Grant, when the moon is at its fullest and there is an electrical storm, this multiplies the effect, causing even more chaos."

I had created my own vortex when I turned on the device. Apparently, I'd been sucked into chaos.

Now I needed more than ever to track down the builder of the device.

We walked back to Jennifer's hotel, talking about the device, the scroll, vortexes and portals. When we got to the lobby, she invited me in.

She *had* said anything.

Her suite was large and plush, the carpet a lime green shag. Wow, flashback!

Before I could sit down, Jennifer said, "Let's take a nice hot shower. You've had a full day and you need to relax."

I stuttered, "That sounds great."

As I slipped off my shoes, I asked her, "Are you staying here by yourself? On vacation?"

Jennifer replied, "Sort of. My family owns the hotel, so I can stay whenever and for as long as I want."

What a dream come true.

She removed her dress and I looked at her and asked, "Am I really here?"

Jennifer laughed. "You already asked me that when we first met. If you ask me again, I really am going to have to smack you!"

At the bathroom door, she turned around. She removed a small gold bracelet with a tiny heart dangling from it and handed it to me. She asked me to put it on the dresser.

I was in such a hurry to get into the shower with her, I tucked the bracelet in my pants pocket instead. Then I took off my pants and left them on the floor.

I had the best shower of my life.

Then I slept like a baby until a crack of thunder woke me up.

It was pouring rain again with loud peals of thunder and huge bolts of lightning. I did not want to get out of bed. I was so warm, and comfortable with Jennifer curled up beside me.

I shook myself. If I was ever going to find the builder of the device, I would have to go now, while the storm was still brewing.

I slipped out of bed in the darkness and got dressed. Then I went in the bathroom and used the light there while I wrote a note to Jennifer. I explained why I had to leave, and promised I would be back.

I left the hotel and ran through the pouring rain to my car. I got in and locked the door. I was soaked to the skin. I pulled out my duffle and reached for the device. Then I turned it on and closed my eyes.

The car shook viciously, followed by a loud blast.

I opened my eyes, and it was nice and sunny outside.

I got out of the car. There were puddles everywhere, the ground soaked from the night before. I looked at the people on the street. I watched the crowds milling about. Everyone was in their own world, glued to their smart phones, walking around with ear buds in. Everybody looked self-absorbed, closed off and defensive.

I was back. It was 2014.

CHAPTER 25

THE BUILDER

I had two messages on my phone from Rod. Len had called too, wondering why I hadn't made it down to his place as planned.

I met up with Len for breakfast and told him about the storm over bagels and cream cheese. I said I fell asleep in the car and woke up there this morning.

He said, "Grant, are you sure someone didn't slip something in your drink last night?"

"I'm sure they didn't because I never made it out of my car, let alone into a bar."

He shook his head, disbelieving. Who could blame him? If I told him I'd spent the night with a girl from 1981, however, he'd think I'd gone around the bend.

Maybe I had.

While we waited for more coffee, I called Rod to see if I could drop by when I got back home.

Rod said, "Sure. If you come over around six, I should be home by then."

I said goodbye to Len and hit the road at noon.

At six o'clock, I drove over to Rod's house. He invited me in and we hung around in his living room chatting. After some mindless conversation, I asked Rod, "So how can I buy one of those meditation devices like the one you loaned me?"

He said, "I knew you'd like it. Well, if you want one, I'll have to call the friend I got it from. Do you want me to call Otto and ask?"

I nodded, so he took out his cell and made the call.

I listened while Rod made conversation, then he asked Otto if he had another mediation device he could sell. He nodded at me and said, "It's for my friend

Grant. I loaned him mine and he loved it so much, he wants his own. I want him to have one so he can give me back the one I loaned him."

He laughed, and then put the phone on speaker. Otto was laughing too.

Otto asked, "No problem. So when do you want to come by and pick it up, Rod?"

I was excited. The mission was moving ahead!

Rod said, "Grant, when do you want to buy it? Now?"

I replied, "I'm ready, I've got my checkbook with me."

Otto interjected, "So Rod, how long have you known this guy?"

Rod looked at me while he spoke. "Oh, not very long. Only about…thirty-seven years."

Otto laughed. "In that case, come on over."

We took Rod's car over to Otto's place. He lived about twenty minutes west, deep in the suburbs.

When we arrived, he was out in the grassy front yard playing with his dog. A small man with perfect muscle tone and no hair, he waved and said, "Hi guys, come on in."

We followed Otto inside the house, your average Florida home with terrazzo floors and a backyard pool and lots of sun. He indicated a rattan couch so we sat down in his comfortable living room.

Otto handed each of us a cold bottle of beer, then disappeared. He returned with another one of the devices in hand. He gave me the device and I turned it on.

I felt the familiar wave of relaxation begin to settle over me. Everything seemed to be in perfect working order.

After I switched it off, I said, "Otto, I'm sold. This little device is awesome!"

He replied, "I know, it really is. There's nothing else on the market like it. At least not that I've ever encountered."

After he told me the price, which was steep, I wrote out a check. When I paid Otto, I asked him if there was an owner's manual with instructions on proper use of the device and information on how it worked.

He looked at me oddly and tilted his head. "Ah, no. Unfortunately, the guy that makes this device does not provide any paperwork with the product. He told me just to demonstrate it to people I think might use it wisely. Most people feel the effects right away and, like you, they're instantly sold. The device actually sells itself."

"Right," I replied, "that's cool. But if I had a question, could I email the guy? Or maybe call him?"

Otto frowned and said, "No. Jesse is aloof. He doesn't usually answer the phone, let alone emails."

He gave Rod a look, and then told us, "Once upon a time, Jesse built things for the military. He had the job for a long time. Now he's retired and doesn't want to be bothered or asked questions about anything."

"I just spent a lot of money on this device. Couldn't I at least write the guy a letter?"

Otto looked at Rod. Rod shrugged.

Otto said, "Well, okay, I'll give you his contact info. But I can't guarantee that he'll get back to you."

"Thanks, I appreciate it."

Otto wrote down the builder's contact information on a slip of paper and handed it to me. I put it away in my wallet for safekeeping.

We stayed a little longer, then returned to Rod's house. I gave Rod back his device and headed for home.

I now had my own device. But did it have the same special contents?

When I got home, I opened up the back. My hand was shaking as I took it apart. Would the scroll be inside?

It looked exactly the same as Rod's device. The coil was there. And the tiny scroll was tucked into place.

The next morning after my second cup of coffee, I typed up a letter to the builder. He lived in the backwoods of Georgia. Not too far away, but most likely another world.

I posted the letter the old fashioned way, and waited anxiously for Jesse's response.

A few weeks went by. Nothing.

A few more weeks went by. Still nothing!

After two months had passed without a response from Jesse, I went to the post office. The postmaster tracked my letter and told me it had been delivered seven weeks before.

It was time for a road trip.

I went home and packed some clothes. I rented a Toyota truck from the rental outfit down the street, filled the tank with gas, and took off for the Blue Ridge Mountains.

Once I got north of West Palm Beach, the roads were no longer crowded. Another in a long line of beautiful days, the morning was sunny, the sky cloudless, and there was a nice warm breeze. I could smell orange groves and pine trees. This was nature at its best.

To my surprise, the Blue Ridge Mountains actually looked blue. This was due to their high content of isoprene, which is a chemical made by the trees that create the beautiful blue haze which envelopes the region.

When I arrived in the town where Jesse lived, I stopped to get a bottle of cold water. I planned to use GPS to find the house. The area was rural, with no signs, lots of land between homes, and dirt roads that led deep into the woods.

I parked at a small convenience store and filled the tank. The few people hanging out front stared as though I might have just crashed landed on earth from another galaxy. I was glad to purchase my water and leave.

When I got back on the road, I turned on satellite navigation and followed the voice navigator and the digital map. I soon found myself on a winding back road. It was desolate, and led me up the side of a steep mountain. The truck moved slowly while driving at a forty-five degree angle. I had to switch gears for more traction.

When I finally reached the top of the mountain, the road flattened out. Up ahead lay a lovely farm with acres of fields and open land. Way at the back on the edge of the woods sat a log cabin. This had to be Jesse's place.

I parked and walked up to the tall iron gate. I peered through but nobody was on the property to let me in. Now I would have to ring the cowbell like the mailman did in order to signify the mail had arrived. But I wasn't the mailman, I wasn't expected, and there was a big sign on the gate that stated: *Owner carries shotgun and will shoot on sight.*

I rang the cowbell several times, with no answer. I sat in the truck, ate some potato chips, had some now tepid water, then got out to ring the cowbell some more. Still no answer.

Back in the truck, I turned on the air conditioning and put on some soothing music. I reclined a bit, cracked the windows to let in the fresh mountain air, and closed my eyes.

Tic, tic, tic.

Someone was knocking on my window with their keys.

I opened my eyes. Outside the passenger side window stood a tall man, a middle-aged guy with graying hair and weathered face.

"Do you mind telling me what you're doing here?" he asked.

"Sure, I'm here to see Jesse," I replied.

"Is Jesse expecting you?" he asked.

"Not really."

"So, what are you doing out here in your truck?"

"Well, I mailed him a letter and waited months for a response. I really needed to speak to him, so here I am."

"What's your name?" he asked.

"My name is Grant Davis."

"Grant, has it ever occurred to you that Jesse doesn't want to be bothered by anyone?"

"Yes," I replied. I knew that. Still, I had to speak to him.

"Looks like you drove a long way to get here. All the way from Florida?"

He'd seen my license plate. "That's right," I replied.

"So is this a life or death emergency?"

"No." I had to admit it wasn't.

"Then what is so important you felt you had to drive all the way to Jesse's house without an invitation?"

"That's what I'm hoping to speak to Jesse about," I replied.

"Is the subject matter of your visit a secret?" he asked.

"Jesse might not want me to tell anyone about it, yes. It's a rather sensitive subject."

He nodded. I felt like I was getting somewhere now.

"If I can get Jesse to come out and speak with you, will you cut to the chase? He has no time or patience to chitchat or figure out riddles."

I nodded. "Yes, sir."

"Okay, stay here. Don't get out of your truck. In fact, don't move."

I nodded again. *Okay.*

He went through a doorway in the iron fence. The gate remained closed. I sat there in the truck, not sure what to expect, as the man walked across the grassy yard to the log cabin. He crossed the porch and disappeared inside.

Chickens clucked and flocked, running around the yard. I felt like one of them, only they still had their heads on straight.

In the distance, goats wandered and cats stretched in the afternoon sun. The barn was big and bright red against the blue of the sky and the deep green of the pine forest.

Suddenly, a disembodied voice announced, "The gates are about to open. Please be careful."

I jumped, and then looked around. The intercom must have been in a fir tree overhead.

After the iron gates folded back out of the way, I carefully drove my truck through. I parked on the dirt drive and walked up to the cabin. I crossed the front porch to a thick wood door and knocked.

JESSE

When the door opened, an old man in his late seventies or early eighties stood in the doorway. He had little hair and a long gray beard. He looked me up and down. "You must be Grant."

"Yes, sir," I replied.

"My son Peter convinced me to let you in. He told me there was a fine gentleman outside who had come a long way just to speak with me."

I nodded.

"Would you like something to drink?"

"Please. Anything cold would be great."

I followed Jesse into the living room and over to a wet bar. He cracked open a can of ginger ale and poured it over ice, then handed the tall glass to me.

"Thank you, sir."

He pointed to a high-back chair and said, "Sit down. Please, tell me. What's on your mind?"

"Can I speak freely, sir?" I asked.

Jesse laughed. "Yes, Grant, this is my house and we speak freely here."

I took a deep breath. "My friend loaned me a device that helps with the process of relaxation," I began.

Jesse was nodding his head and smiling. He said, "Yes, go on."

"This device, it works really well. I should restate that, sir. It's amazing! It's the most amazing device I've ever experienced in my life!"

His smile widened. "I'm glad you like it. But, that's not why you drove all the way here, is it? Just to tell me you like my little invention?"

"No, there's more to it than that. I needed to find the builder. I had to find you, in fact."

And I told him about the drive to Miami, the full moon, the storm, and using the device on the side of the road. He stared at me, his blue eyes intelligent and warm. He seemed so understanding, so accepting, that I told him about Jennifer, my too modern clothes, and the newspaper that said it was May 19, 1981.

I finished my story by adding, "And I loved the eighties, by the way. The best era ever!"

Jesse chortled as he filled a pipe with cherry tobacco. After a moment, he said, "Grant, have you told anyone about this experience of yours?"

"Not really," I said.

He lit the pipe and inhaled. Then he stared into my eyes and said in a serious tone, "Do not tell anyone about your experience. Do not mention it to anyone. Not ever. Do you understand?"

Oops. I had already told Jennifer. But she was there, in the funky Fontainebleau hotel, version 1981. So by now she would be thirty-three years older and I was way, way in her past.

"Yes, I understand," I replied.

"Grant, where did you get the device?"

"Well, from my friend Rod. He got it from a yoga instructor named Otto."

Jesse smiled and sucked on his pipe. "Otto? Oh, he's a good kid. I've known his father for nearly fifty years."

He sat back, relaxed, the smoke drifting up to encircle his head. "These devices have almost magical properties. Inside of each of them, I've wrapped a mystical scroll around the antenna coil. By doing so, the device unlocks all kinds of doorways. My wife, you see, she studied mysticism."

He looked at a painting on the wall of an older woman with long dark hair.

"The scroll releases good throughout the universe and into the life of the person using the device. And when there is a full moon, all of the vortexes and portals open up."

I nodded. "Someone told me that recently."

Jesse smiled and waved his hand in the air. "My boy, everyone knows that! I knew about portals when I was knee high to a grasshopper."

I shrugged. "Well, it sure seems like everybody knew about this portal stuff but me."

Jesse said, "So there was a full moon, coupled with an electrical storm. You were right on the edge of the Bermuda Triangle, and the phase of the open portal and the phase of the device must've synced up. The two converged, creating some type of wormhole and causing you to travel back in time or into some parallel universe where 1981 still exists."

Huh? Had I? Really?

I must have looked shocked because Jesse leaned forward and patted my knee. "Grant, these things aren't as uncommon as you might think. It's just that people don't talk about it when it happens to them."

And I could understand why. Who would believe them? Who would believe me?

"I was dressed all wrong. I stood out like a sore thumb. I had to run to a thrift shop to get some clothes to wear so I could fit in. What if someone saw my cell phone? What would they have thought?"

"It sounds like you managed okay," Jesse replied with a smile.

"I did. And I met a wonderful girl. Her family owned the hotel."

"Take me with you next time. I want to find a girl whose family owns a hotel too."

We both laughed.

"How am I ever going to see her again?" I asked him.

I thought I had wanted to discover the secret to the device, the secret to the Vedic Sanskrit symbols, the secret to achieving perfect harmony and wellness for all. Instead, what I most wanted was to find Jennifer again. I wanted to go back to the eighties.

"How? I don't know," Jesse replied with a shrug. "Nobody ever asked me that before."

He puffed on his pipe. We sat in silence for a few minutes.

"Wait a second, Grant. Were you listening to the car radio when all of this took place?"

"Yes, the radio was on," I replied.

"What song was playing when you turned on the device? Do you remember?" Jesse asked.

"Let me think…Oh! Yes, I do remember the song! 'Right Here, Right Now'.

One of my favorites. But I liked music in the eighties the best. Back then, people really strived to make good music. Music came from the soul. It wasn't created just for the money. The music had more feeling to it and the songs had substance and meaning."

Jesse nodded. "That song? That's one key you can try to use. Do you have anything of the girl's? Something you might've brought back with you?"

"Funny you should ask me that. When I was doing my laundry yesterday, I found something of hers. I have Jennifer's bracelet at my house, tucked away somewhere safe."

Jesse said, "So that's what you'll use to get back there to see her again. Both the song and the bracelet, coupled with the device, should get you back there with her. Provided you can sync up with another portal. And an electrical storm in Miami." Jesse laughed and said, "But you'll have to wait until a full moon. Then I'd suggest you park your car in Miami, turn on the device, play the song, hold the bracelet, and think of Jennifer. If all the energies are aligned correctly, you should find yourself with her again."

"How do you know that?" I asked.

"I already told you, these things aren't as uncommon as you might think."

"So you've time travelled before too?" I asked.

"Oh yes. After all, I *am* the builder. Right?" He laughed the smoke swirling about his head like a halo.

"What else can I use your device for?" I asked. "It didn't come with an owner's manual."

"Grant, it's all about intention. When you have the right intent, the desire within you, and the device, then many, many, wonderful things are possible. Things that didn't seem possible before. Know what I mean?"

I laughed. "Of course. And I'm living proof of that."

Jesse stood up. "It's getting late. Do you have a place to stay for the evening?"

"No, not yet."

"Well, I have a guestroom you may stay in, just for tonight," he said.

"Thank you, sir."

"Okay, but you'll have to stop sir-ing me. Call me Jesse."

I laughed and said okay.

After Peter led me to the guest room, I thanked him and retired for the night.

CHAPTER 26

BACK TO THE FUTURE

I awoke to the fine aroma of grilled sausages.

When I came out of the guest room, Jesse was at the stove. "Good morning! You have a long ride ahead of you, Grant, so you're going to need something substantial in your belly."

"Thank you, Jesse, I appreciate your hospitality."

"Have a seat and I'll bring the food to the table." He was stirring the eggs.

After he refused my offer to assist, I sat down. Peter wasn't around.

Jesse brought over plates of steaming scrambled eggs, thick pancakes, and plump sausages. He said, "The eggs are from my girls out in the yard. The syrup on the table I tapped from the trees out there too."

"Everything looks so good," I said.

"Well, start eating, then."

After breakfast, I said, "Jesse that was superb. Give my compliments to the chef."

We both laughed.

Jesse put on a pot of coffee and sat down with me while it was brewing.

"Jesse, I'm curious. How did you ever come up with the idea for the device?"

He smiled, sat back in his chair. "I was in the service during the Vietnam War. After that, I contracted as an engineer for many years within a division of our government. When I say many years, what I really mean is most of my life. All of my projects were defense related. I never worked on anything else."

He looked at me intently and I nodded. That had to be hard.

"Well, after I retired, I decided I wanted to build something that could help bring happiness and a sense of comfort and relaxation to people. I had paid my dues, now I wanted to make something that healed rather than destroyed. For the first time in my life, I would create something not for war, but for peace."

He got up to pour the coffee.

"When I started creating the schematics for the device I had in mind, my intention was to help my buddies who had been traumatized in Vietnam. My friends who were veterans, many of them still struggling with issues leftover from the war. Once I finished the schematics, I began building. The first model was good, but it needed some work, it needed to be tweaked."

He brought over the cups of coffee, then a pitcher of cream and a crystal bowl of sugar.

"When I created the second model, I made all the necessary adjustments to the device from within the schematics. Then I showed my wife the device. Betty liked it and all, but she said to me, 'Jesse, you found the right frequency to help people relax and feel at ease, but don't you want more than that? You want to add depth, richness, and love to people's lives, along with those feelings of relaxation, comfort, and that wonderful sense of peace.' And damn, she was right. I didn't know how to do that, though. She suggested I accompany her to her yoga class."

He laughed and raised his bushy eyebrows.

"I went with her to the class at a local meditation center. I tried some of the meditation techniques they were teaching and found the practice to be quite powerful. I overheard some of the women in my wife's class talking about how they had changed their lives since they'd started practicing yoga. The whole experience was an eye opener for me."

I sipped my coffee. I was well aware of the power of meditation. And yoga.

"Betty introduced me to a friend. Ileana offered to lend me some books and teach me some of the core principles of meditation. I took her up on her offer. Betty and I went to Ileana's house, and that's where we learned about the scroll. Ileana had a copy she'd transcribed from an old book on Sanskrit wisdoms. She gave me a copy and I tucked it in my pocket."

"Wow!" I said. "Isn't it amazing how things just fall into place sometimes?"

"It is. Serendipity. So that night, Betty said to me, 'Are you thinking what I'm thinking?' and I said, 'It all depends on what you're thinking.'"

I laughed.

"My wife and I agreed to mediate together with my device turned on. Then Betty suggested we include the scroll Ileana had given us. So I figured out a way to work it into the device."

"How did you do that? Was Ileana's copy of the scroll that small?"

He shook his head. "No, but that evening I made the smallest version of the scroll I could design so that it fit snugly inside the device. Then we just hoped for the best."

He poured more coffee in my cup, his face pink with excitement.

"And Grant, the best is what we got! The more we used the device, the better our lives became. Soon after that, we moved here and began to lead the life we'd always dreamed about."

He looked at me. "She loved it here, my wife. I miss her terribly."

"You must. She sounds like a wise woman. And this place is fantastic. Your device is amazing. You've done so much for your life, and for the lives of others. Including mine." I held out my hand.

We shook hands and I stood up to leave.

"Thank you so much, Jesse. For a delicious breakfast. For sharing your stories with me. For your invention. For everything. Now I'd better hit the road."

"I enjoyed your company; it's been an unexpected pleasure. Keep in touch, son."

I said I would do so.

Peter appeared from somewhere on the farm and opened the gate for me. I waved and drove off.

The mountains were blue and clear. The road seemed endless, the trees plush, the air fresh and clean. The drive was scenic and relaxing.

I needed to call Dr. Siegfried and ask him about all that I had learned from the builder of the device.

I pulled over to the side of the road and took out my cell. Then I snapped a photo of the device, including the tiny scroll tucked inside. I sent it to Dr. Siegfried.

A few hours later I was on the interstate when my phone rang. Dr. Siegfried. We chatted for a moment and caught up. Neither of us mentioned Ursula. The pain of that relationship had diminished. She was not the woman for me. Jennifer was. Unfortunately, Jennifer was still living in 1981.

When I asked what he thought of the photos I had sent, Dr. Siegfried said, "Grant, it looks to me like this device can produce phase conjugation. That is, a time reversed wave that travels backwards and converges, creating a particle as well as a photonic exchange within the flux at a rate where the potential can reach infinity."

I didn't want to interrupt him. He sounded excited. But huh?

"This means extraordinary electromagnetic anomalies exist within dynamic equations that far surpass the capacity of vectors and tensors. Within this mechanism, a vacuum is created that's not necessarily confined by the speed of light, thus causing time travel phenomena."

"Dr. Siegfried, speak to me in layman's terms, please," I begged.

He laughed. "Look, what was once a dream is now a reality. Time travel exists."

"But Dr. Siegfried, how do you explain the scroll?"

"I can only say the scroll is where science and magic intertwine to become a latticework of infinite energy. Where the scope of theory becomes that of reality. Ultimately, Grant, that scroll in that device of yours is the universal passport to parallel universes."

We agreed to discuss the device in more detail when I was no longer driving. Dr. Siegfried wanted more photos, and he said he also needed a sample. He wanted me to get him one of the devices so that he could analyze it in his lab.

We talked for a while but I was hesitant to make plans. Did I want to return to Bavaria?

On my way home, I decided to stop at the Kabbalah Center. It was not yet dusk when I pulled into the parking lot.

Marc greeted me and went to get David while I took a seat in the lobby. Marc returned and asked me to follow him inside. We joined David in a glass conference room lined with leather office chairs. After shaking hands, we sat around a large mahogany table sipping on ice water.

Without revealing Jesse's identity, I told them why the device had been built. I attempted to explain how it worked. I also explained how, when someone's intent was for the good, the device was able to shift reality and steer destiny in a new direction.

David nodded. He said, "Fascinating stuff, Grant. From our understanding, this means your builder friend created a device that elicits peace and harmony with a frequency that has always been a blanket for this earth. The blanket has served as the natural signaling guide for not only our own biology, but for the biology of every living creature that inhabits the earth."

Marc interjected, "The man who designed the device went beyond the normal limits by placing the scroll strategically within the device, adding a separate instrument to amplify the 'open sesame' quality of his device."

David added, "Marc, correct me if I'm wrong. You're saying that the scroll is the source code and the device is the amplifier?"

Marc nodded.

I said, "It seems like you can use each component separately with remarkable results, but together, synergistically, this device can create a universe in the eye of the beholder, a new realm far greater than the one we normally access. The possibilities are endless!"

"This device is helping to do the Almighty's work," David added.

Marc and I nodded.

RIGHT HERE, RIGHT NOW

I left the Center as darkness seeped across the sky. I was tired from the long day, and I had a lot on my mind.

When I got to the condo, I was tapped out. I skipped dinner and my usual rituals and lay down on the bed. My body was exhausted but my mind reeled.

I thought about my own future, now that I had access to the device and information about what it was capable of doing. I could create a business and sell the device to improve lives and help countless people—and animals—heal. I could time travel and see history, see the future. I could go back to the eighties and be with Jennifer. With the knowledge I had acquired throughout the years since 1981, I could prevent catastrophes from occurring. I might introduce the formula to help reduce suffering and enhance well-being in the 1980s and beyond.

If I went back to the past, no government agents or idiots from my old neighborhood would be after me. My life would be peaceful, yet fulfilling. I could help to shape a better future than the one I was living in. Better for me, better for everyone else.

Or I could head for Bavaria and work with Dr. Siegfried on the device. Maybe introduce Jesse to the German doctor so that the two geniuses could devise new ways to promote time travel and introduce an era of world peace.

I didn't know what to do. I tossed and turned until eventually I fell into a fitful sleep.

When I woke up, I was on the couch. The sun was up and I could hear the birds chirping. Then a new sound emerged from the bedroom.

Clunk, drag, clunk, drag.

What the hell was that?

A booming voice called out "Good morning!"

AUTHOR'S NOTE

You may be wondering how much of my story is fiction and how much is fact.

My answer to you is yes and …Yes!

Now you've read my life story from the early day's right up to the current day.

I cannot confirm or deny any of the material presented.

But within these pages, the realms of possibilities for fact as well as fiction collide, reaching the zero point on the metaphysical titer scale of life.

This is where a wonderful secret opening can be created within our vacuum of existence.

By the way …I Okayed This!

ABOUT THE AUTHOR:

The author, Philip E. Barrington, is originally from New York City. He worked in luxury goods at the "Jewel" of Manhattan. He now resides in beautiful, warm and sunny south Florida, where he taps into his creativity side to write.